Campbell del Rio
DREAMS OF YOU

THE LOTUS CIRCLE

A The Lotus Circle Publication

www.thelotuscircle.com

Dreams of You

ISBN # 9781419980008
Edited by Kelli Kwiatkowski
Cover art by Darrell King

Electronic book Publication April 2007
Trade Paperback Publication April 2007

About the Authors

❧

Campbell del Rio is the pseudonym of the mother-daughter writing team of Marilyn Campbell and Joie del Rio.

Besides her established profession as a multi-genre, best-selling fiction author, Marilyn Campbell is a screenwriter, motivational speaker and business consultant. She is also a life-long student of metaphysics whose natural intuition was strongly enhanced following a near-death experience. She is now focused on sharing with her readers all the wonderful things she learned on "The Other Side".

Joie del Rio's imagination never takes a rest. Even in her sleep, she often dreams of tales of adventure or romance, but she has plenty of grounding influence in her life as well. The daughter of a veteran police officer, she is currently a history major and is married to a real-life American hero currently serving in the Army Medical Corps.

The authors welcome comments from readers. You can find their website and email address on her author bio page at www.thelotuscircle.com

Author Note

※

Dear Reader,

Welcome to the World of The Lotus Circle! We are extremely happy to bring you the first novel about one of the gifted descendants of that ancient secret society. For more information, go to www.thelotuscircle.com.

We are doubly excited because this is the first collaborative effort of the mother-and-daughter writing team of Marilyn Campbell and Joie del Rio. We hope you enjoy reading this tale as much as we enjoyed creating it.

Best wishes,
Campbell del Rio

DREAMS OF YOU

ॐ

Dedication

❧

This book is dedicated to Julio del Rio, our own real-life hero, for his patience and support while his wife and mother-in-law paid more attention to this book than to him.

Trademarks Acknowledgement

❧

The author acknowledges the trademarked status and trademark owners of the following wordmarks mentioned in this work of fiction:

Carnaval Miami: Kiwanis Club of Little Havana, Inc.

Super Bowl: National Football League

Chapter One

"Help me. Please. Somebody..." The deep, male voice is more frustrated than fearful...his face becomes clear but surrounded by thick gray fog...chiseled features, strong jaw, dark hair, dark eyes, medium complexion, mid to late thirties...he glances from side to side as though worried that he'll be overheard... "I've got to get out of here."

Leilani Wakefield reached for the pad and pen on her nightstand without opening her eyes or turning on the light. Recording certain dreams without completely waking up had taken a lot of practice, but it was now a regular part of her nightly routine. Using a type of shorthand she developed for the purpose, she made her notes and was sound asleep a minute later.

It was also Leilani's habit to awaken at sunrise and transcribe her notes before the curtain between her conscious and subconscious mind closed for the day. This morning there were two dreams that felt meaningful. The first she interpreted easily because it concerned one of the questions she had posed before going to sleep.

But the second — in which a man was pleading for help — that one would need more thought. It had a very different feel and look, unlike anything in her regular dream categories. The face seemed very familiar, however, as though she should know him, but on a conscious level she was certain that she did not.

Once the new dreams were added to her journal, it was review time. Every morning, she sat down at her kitchen table with her dream journal, the daily newspaper and the television news channel droning in her ear. From time to time, she would read or hear something relevant to a dream she'd had, then she would make a notation beside it in her journal. Although that much concentrated news was sometimes depressing, a very large mug of hot coffee helped it go down more easily.

Tracking the news was a necessary part of interpreting the predictive dreams that had no previous frame of reference. Sometimes her interpretation came too late to do anything about a coming event, yet she would note it in her journal for future reference. On the other hand, she sometimes figured out the warning in time to help. To do that, however, she needed a friend on the local police department who knew she wasn't crazy.

Satisfied that there were no clues in the news about the man, or any other pending dreams, she called her friend Neil Foster to tell him what she had learned in her dreamtime. When she'd first met Neil, he was a sergeant with the Brevard County Sheriff's Department and he'd been totally skeptical of a warning she gave him. Five years later, Neil was now a captain on the force, a complete believer in her extrasensory abilities and a very good friend.

He answered his cell phone on the second ring. "Hold on a sec."

Leilani heard him tell his wife to go back to sleep, then there was the soft click of a door closing before he spoke to her again.

"Sorry about that. Both kids are sick with some kind of stomach thing, so we were up most of the night. It's times like this that I can understand why you're in no hurry to get tied down. Okay, I'm ready. A sunrise call from you can only mean one thing." His tone instantly grew wary. "Do I need to sit down?"

She laughed, knowing that nothing she said really shocked him anymore. "No. This was a mild one. It's about the missing bicycle." From time to time, she would go to his office and skim over a few reports on cases where the investigator had come to a dead end. This was just one of dozens she had looked at yesterday. "You said you were worried about it triggering some neighborhood violence."

"Yeah. An accusation was tossed out and the war drums started beating."

"You were right about that. It felt important to solve it as soon as possible. Anyway, I saw a child, not big enough to be a teenager, in jeans and a hooded blue sweatshirt, pushing the bike into a garage. I couldn't see anything else about the child. It was dark out, but the street lights helped me see the house pretty clearly and there was a light over the front door that let me see the number on it, but I couldn't see a street sign." She described the house and front yard well enough for someone to identify it, *if* they could find the right street. "I'm sorry I couldn't see more, but the dream was connected to the bicycle. Once the garage door was closed, my view was blacked out."

"Well, it's more than we had before. Thanks, pal. You'll have to come over for barbecue again, after the kids are better."

"I'd like that...as long as you promise not to try to fix me up with any more of your cop friends."

"What? Hello? You're cutting out."

"Very funny. Try not to work too hard today."

Like a lot of people, Leilani had personal "problem solving" dreams in which a daytime dilemma sorted itself out while she slept. Sometimes all this took was being relaxed enough to let go of the worries surrounding a problem to *see* what had been hidden by the conscious thought processes.

What was different from most people's dreamtime, however, was that she could focus on *other* people's problems before going to sleep and awaken with a piece of information or bit of advice. As with the missing bicycle, one problem might be more important than the others, in which case it tended to push other questions aside.

But it hadn't pushed aside the dream about the man.

Alternatively, the solutions to some problems stayed out of her reach no matter how strongly or how often she focused on them. Grandma had taught her that these were ones that she was not permitted to interfere with, either due to fate or an individual's need to learn a lesson on his or her own.

Something Leilani had learned on her own was that she couldn't live entirely in the dream world. Her body and her conscious mind needed regular exercise. After clearing the kitchen table, she got dressed to take her daily walk. With sunscreen on her face and her straight black hair gathered up under her favorite ball cap, she stepped out of her front door to greet the day.

As she stretched her leg muscles, she took her usual moment to be grateful. The Florida sun kissed her skin and she inhaled the salty, humid air coming to her on an ocean breeze. It was the middle of February. Her father and stepmother were probably shoveling snow out of their Pennsylvania driveway about now. Her brother and his wife would be bundling up the kids to go to their grade school in Ohio. And here she was…walking to the beach in lightweight yoga pants and a tank top.

Leilani considered her life to be quite perfect, but her circumstances had not come about haphazardly. Her dreams gave her ideas and, with complete faith that the universe had a plan, she acted on them. Many happy years with Grandma on the Big Island of Hawaii convinced her that she never wanted to live far from the ocean. After her grandmother passed away, she had a dream of the sun rising instead of setting over the ocean, so Leilani decided to give the Atlantic a try. With her inheritance, she opened The Treasure Chest, a small book and gift store in the historic section of Melbourne, Florida.

This morning did not allow for an extended walk. She and her sole employee, Tillie, took turns opening The Treasure Chest, and since today was Monday, it was her turn. A creature of habit, by eight-thirty Leilani was showered, dressed and driving to the store.

The fact that there was a customer waiting to get in when she arrived twenty minutes later was a sure sign of a busy day ahead. That sign turned out to be so accurate that she gave Tillie an extra-long hug when she arrived at two o'clock. "Thank goodness you're here!"

Tillie's eyes widened at the sight of all the customers then narrowed again when she saw the dozen large boxes that had been delivered and were partially blocking one aisle. "You've got to be kidding. What's all this?"

"I'm not sure," Leilani said, turning back to the cash register to check out a customer. "I haven't even had time to look at the return addresses. But I'm guessing at least some of them contain the birthday gift mugs we agreed to take on consignment."

"Hmph. Maybe we'll get lucky and each box only has one mug in it, surrounded by lots and lots of bubble wrap! Okay, I guess I better tackle that first."

"Actually, I would really like to get out from behind this counter for a while. Would you mind?"

Tillie laughed. "In other words, you're afraid the old lady might hurt herself trying to move the boxes around."

"That might be true if there was an old lady here. The truth is I've got to figure out what to rearrange first, regardless of what's in the boxes."

Tillie accepted her explanation, though they both knew that her age and arthritis had everything to do with Leilani's task assignments. Although Tillie's body was nearing eighty, her mind was as sharp as ever and Leilani had no idea how she would ever manage without her.

Tillie had entered the store as a customer the first month it opened and, by the second month, she accepted Leilani's offer to help her out one or two days a week. As the years passed, Tillie's hours kept increasing until she was there almost as much as her boss. Leilani counted on her lighthearted logic as much as her dependability and Tillie treated her like the daughter she never had. The arrangement and relationship were just two more perfect aspects of Leilani's life.

"Excuse me."

Leilani turned toward the male voice and smiled at the customer who had been browsing for over an hour. This was at least the third time he'd done so in the last couple weeks. As she had with every man she saw that day, she took a good look at his eyes, just to make sure it wasn't the man from her dream. The browser was definitely not that man, and yet there was something about him that seemed familiar as well. Besides that, he was standing so close she felt the need to take a step back before answering. "Can I help you find something?"

He cleared his throat, shifted his weight from one foot to the other and focused on a spot behind her. "Um, yes, please. I was wondering if you had a book on white-water rafting."

The request seemed so contradictory to his quiet, late middle-aged, slightly rounded appearance that it took her a moment to reply. She led him to the travel section and pointed out a book on adventurous traveling and camping. As she returned to her project, she felt his gaze following her. He seemed to want to say something else, but her instincts prevented her from encouraging him.

Leilani stuck around until the store emptied out a bit so that she and Tillie could have their daily chat over tea and cookies. "Did you see that man who hung around for so long again today?"

"You mean Randy Krupp?"

Leilani laughed. "When did you get his name?"

"He used a credit card, and you know I always try to remember the names of regulars."

"Yes, he does seem to be turning into a regular customer, doesn't he?"

Tillie arched an eyebrow. "Regular, yes. Customer, not so much. Oh, he buys something every time he's here, but what he wants isn't for sale."

"Spill, woman. What do you know about Mr. Krupp?"

"Not much. Just that he looks at you like you're the homecoming queen and he's the class nerd. My guess is that he would really like to get to know you, but he's much too shy."

"I sort of got that feeling but..." She still hadn't quite put her finger on what the "but" was about the man.

Tillie gave her a moment before prodding. "Talk it through, baby. Isn't that what your grandma used to say? You know it won't go any further than these old ears. I'll probably forget it by tonight anyway."

"Stop that," Leilani scolded with a smile. "Anybody who memorizes customers' names off their credit cards, no matter how busy we are, then remembers to greet them by name a week later is *not* getting senile." She mentally shifted gears to find a starting place. "I had a different kind of dream last night and it's got me a little bugged. It's been years since that's happened."

"What do you mean 'different'?"

"Not like any of the others. It felt important, not like a throw-away and — "

"Wait. It's been a while since you explained this dream stuff to me. What's a throw-away?"

"I call them that because they're like housekeeping for your brain. They clean out useless stuff collected during the day. This one felt like I was remote-viewing. You know, seeing something as it was happening, but in another place. And then there was something else, something familiar about the man in this dream, even though I'm certain I don't know him. All I saw was his face and he was pleading for help."

"Maybe he's a celebrity of some sort, or a politician, and you've seen his face on television."

"Always possible, but I can usually recognize that kind of thing. Like I said, this had a different feel to it. And then when I looked Mr. Krupp in the eyes, I got a similar feeling of knowing him from somewhere."

Tillie's forehead creased with thought. "What did you mean about it being years since this happened? Maybe that's a clue."

"I don't think so. I just meant it's been a long time since I had a completely new type of dream. While Grandma was around, all I had to do was ask her and she had all the answers. Now I pretty much have to figure out new stuff through trial and error. Hopefully I'll figure it out before it's too late for that poor man, but there's just no telling when that will happen."

"Now don't you start buying worries over that man. The problem he's wanting to be rescued from could be nothing more than a low-paying job or a bad relationship."

"Hmmm. Could be, but it felt more important and— *Oh my!* I just realized something. Instead of my usual *watching* the dream, like an audience watches a movie, it felt like he was talking directly to me. Like *he* was watching *me*!" She gave Tillie another big hug. "Thank you so much. Grandma couldn't have helped me any better."

Tillie waved away the praise. "All I did was stand here while you talked."

"Yes, but *you* told me to talk it through. Okay, now I can go home. I'll see you tomorrow." With one more happy hug, Leilani was on her way.

The drive home was another pleasant part of her day, mainly because half of it was along the beach. Today, because of her conversation with Tillie, her driving time was filled with memories of Grandma.

Leilani was fairly sure that she had been a lucid dreamer all of her thirty-one years, but it wasn't until she turned ten that it was explained to her. During the week before that birthday, she had a series of dreams about her mother being sick and dying. They seemed so real that she would wake up crying every time. When her maternal grandmother called to wish her a happy birthday, she asked Leilani if she was upset about something.

Leilani was named after her grandmother but had not known that she'd inherited a unique ability from her as well. The elder Leilani encouraged the child to talk it through and that became the first session of many she would spend under the tutelage of the wise woman. Having lived nearly seven decades with a strong sense of intuition and the ability to see future events in her dreams, Grandma had a lot to teach her about the gift of lucid dreaming.

Because of Leilani's dreams about her mother, Grandma came for an extended visit and convinced her daughter to get a checkup. The tests indicated the presence of cancer. By finding it in the early stages, she received immediate treatment and for several years it looked like they had beaten it.

However, when Leilani was fifteen the disease came back, and this time the dream came true. Sharing her dream had only delayed the prediction, but it had prolonged the time she had with her mother and made her more grateful for every moment of it.

After the funeral, her father agreed to let her go live with Grandma in Hawaii. Over the next ten years, with her grandmother's help, Leilani learned how to make the most of her gift. By recording every dream and how it felt, then comparing it to things that happened in her daily life, she was able to create a glossary of images that repeatedly meant the same thing.

Similar to the dream that led her to Florida's east coast, another one guided her to the perfect house.

Two years ago, she had a dream about a man named Patrick. He was pointing to fighter jets circling in an arrow formation over the ocean. Before going to sleep, she had focused on finding a home she could buy within reasonable driving distance of her store. Thus, she interpreted the images to be a suggestion to take a ride to Patrick Air Force Base, less than a half hour north. To her delight, she found herself in a neighborhood of old, reasonably priced homes, within walking distance of the Atlantic Ocean.

The one she bought was in need of some major renovation, but she soon discovered that she was pretty good at home repairs. As she pulled into her driveway, she noticed how high the grass was and decided that the yard needed to be taken care of before she could continue her current project of refinishing the kitchen cabinets.

"Lay-lay!"

"Guess what!"

Leilani held out her arms as the excited little girls ran toward her. Instead of catching them for a group hug, however, she was knocked to the ground, causing a group tickle fest. "I give up!" Leilani cried, but it still took a while to get them to calm down. "You two are getting soooo strong. I wouldn't be surprised if you end up becoming champion wrestlers!" That triggered a new round of giggles.

"That's silly," five-year-old Nina stated firmly. "I'm going to be a doctor."

As usual, her four-year-old sister Maddy was much more open-minded. "Do westlers make lotsa money?"

Leilani pretended to give that some serious thought. "I'm not sure about that, but I bet they have more fun than doctors."

"Then I'm gonna be a westler when I gwow up!"

Leilani could just picture Ali's face when she heard that proclamation. She and the girls' mother had hit it off the day she moved in next door to the young family. Leilani enjoyed the girls enough to watch them whenever the regular sitter was unavailable. In return, Ali made sure Leilani never had a shortage of cookies to take into the store.

After a bit more silliness, Leilani asked, "So what's the big news?" That question instigated an argument about who would get to tell Lay-lay, but as usual, Nina won, sort of.

"Mommy said we could get a cat—"

"If we can keep our room clean for a whole month," Maddy finished, grabbing the spotlight from her sister.

"A whole month?" Leilani asked skeptically. "Isn't that, like, *forever* at your age? Listen, I need to mow the grass before it gets dark. How about if you two pick up your toys so I don't accidentally run over them?"

The thought of what a lawn mower could do to their possessions nudged the girls into action and gave Leilani an easy getaway. A few minutes later, she was back outside in her yard work outfit. The smell of newly cut grass was another one of her favorite things in life.

Yes, her life was almost perfect. Actually, until three months ago, she thought her life was *completely* perfect. She didn't even know she was missing something very important.

But that was before she discovered The Lotus Circle...or rather, it discovered her.

The sun was starting to set as Leilani pushed the lawn mower back into the garage and put away the other yard tools. Although her hands had been busy with making her yard perfect again, her mind kept mulling over the one imperfect piece of her life.

Three months ago, she had a dream about a woman selling a book. The very next day, she received an email about a national wellness conference to be held in Sedona, Arizona. Curious, she went to the website and saw pictures of the speakers, one of whom was Dr. Olivia Crandall—the woman in her dream. Without a moment's hesitation, Leilani signed up to attend.

She had thought it sounded interesting. She had not expected it to reveal that she was a descendant of an ancient secret society.

Chapter Two

"It's too late. I'm trapped. There's no way I can get out of here now." The same man's voice and face...more worried now...the features less clear...fog beginning to close in...his eyes squinting to see... *"Whoever you are, please hurry. Find me. There's not much time left."*

Leilani woke up with her heart pounding as though in a state of panic, not a normal reaction for her. She was used to remaining unaffected by her dreams, even the nightmarish ones. But this felt so personal. The man was looking right at *her*, begging *her* to help him. Not only did the brief dream now have more urgency to it, he seemed to be anticipating someone's...no, not someone's...*her* imminent arrival to rescue him.

That simply made no sense. She never got personally involved in the follow-up of a dream. She passed on the warning or advice then let it go. Even in the case of her mother, she only passed the information on to her grandmother to deal with. Perhaps if she had any idea who he was, if she had some sort of intimate connection to him, she might understand the sense of compulsion to do something more. But this man was a complete stranger. She was certain of it.

Or was she?

She reached for her notepad and was more frustrated when she saw that she had only scribbled out two words in all caps—HELP ME.

If she had any other dreams that night, they were all blocked out by this one. She tried to perform her regular morning routine but it was no use. Instead of being able to let it go as soon as she wrote out the details, his words kept replaying in her head. She managed to pour herself a cup of coffee, but as she skimmed the newspaper, the words all blurred together and the television news sounded like gibberish.

Finally she stopped trying to force her routine. The Universe was clearly sending a message—*nothing is as important as finding that man*.

She took a deep breath and made herself relax. Slowly, she quieted all the noise in her head and called on the one person she could always count on, in this or any other dimension.

Grandma? Can you hear me? I really could use some help on this one.

Nothing.

Could you at least give me a clue or show me a sign, anything to help me figure this out?

For whatever reason, Grandma wasn't jumping in on this one. Leilani knew that was important, she just didn't know why. Just as she was about to give up, a sweet floral scent wafted by. She opened her eyes, half expecting a bouquet of flowers to be under her nose, but nothing had been added to her room. Another sniff confirmed that it wasn't her imagination. It was strong, almost like a perfume. The word *aphrodisiac* popped into her head and she smiled. "Thanks, Grandma. I got the message."

The heavy, sweet smell was a characteristic of the lotus flower, once believed to have been an aphrodisiac. Grandma seemed to be reminding her that she was not the only source of spiritual wisdom available. Leilani had not yet taken advantage of being a member of the heart of The Lotus Circle but apparently it was time to acknowledge her heritage.

A few months ago, when she attended the conference in Sedona, she had made sure to attend Dr. Crandall's workshop. The lecture was about the universal laws of synchronicity and attraction. It was all quite illuminating. What sent a shiver down Leilani's spine, however, was the part concerning an ancient secret society known as The Lotus Circle. Afterward, she and another attendee, Ursula Milkovilch, both approached the speaker for more information about the group.

Olivia explained that The Lotus Circle was once a powerful group of women with extrasensory gifts. These gifts and the knowledge of the Circle were handed down from mothers to daughters over the centuries. Gradually, however, the threads were broken as the members were repressed, punished, and forced into secrecy by fearful men and organized religions.

In order to bring The Lotus Circle back into the light for the benefit of the world, it was necessary to gather five descendants of the original Circle to rebuild its heart. For nearly a year, Olivia had been traveling around the globe without encountering any of the women she sought. By the end of the Sedona conference, however, she had accomplished her goal.

Aside from being an accredited parapsychologist, Olivia was a medium, with the ability to communicate with beings of other dimensions. Leilani's lucid dreaming ability qualified her, even though she had no recollection of The Lotus Circle. Ursula was a successful astrologer whose grandmother had told her about the Circle. Temperance Rey, known as Rainy, had been instructed about the ancient society and trained to read Tarot cards by her mother. The fifth member, who was still a bit of a mystery to Leilani, was an empathic healer named Sadira. If their coming together had not been synchronistic enough, the initials of their first names spelled LOTUS, and Sadira was Persian for lotus tree.

Leilani logged onto The Lotus Circle website and entered the private chat room for the five members of the heart. She felt it was a good sign when she saw that Rainy was already logged in and quickly sent her an instant message.

L: Hi Rainy. Leilani here. I could use a reading if you have a few minutes.

T: Hey there. Good to hear from you for any reason. I have time now. Whazzup?

Leilani gave her a brief overview of the dream and why it was bothering her.

L: I feel like I have to do something asap, but I have no idea what.

T: I drew three overview cards as you typed. All were Major Arcana, meaning a big issue in your life. The first identifies the current situation. You got The Moon, which refs your dreamtime but also suggests a big mystery that you need to shed light on.

L: No surprise there.

T: The second shows obstacles in your path. You got Justice. It symbolizes legal situations and balance, but it also suggests a karmic issue.

L: Explain pls.

T: Like maybe the man is someone from a past life. Could be why he seems familiar but not.

Leilani laughed to herself. She couldn't figure out men in her present life. How was she supposed to deal with one who wasn't even in the same realm?

L: And the third?

T: Outcome. Wheel of Fortune. Big change in your life and his. But I also feel like it's bigger than that.

L: I'm still confused.

T: I just pulled one more card to clarify the outcome. It's The World. Whatever you need to do for him could have global implications.

L: Swell. Nothing like a little pressure.

T: The key is the Justice card. You need to look at the karma.

L: But it felt like he's in the present, not the past.

T: Maybe his current incarnation is about to enter your life and the dream was to make sure you notice him.

L: You mean like a repeat engagement?

T: Maybe. Or a chance to do it better. Or it might not be him personally. Maybe something happened with him in a previous life that has relevance to a present situation.

L: That's a lot of possibilities. I suppose I could pose a question about a past life with this man before I go to sleep tonight.

T: You could try, but I think you need a regression therapist. The Lotus Circle has about a thousand members already. Surely one of them does past-life work. Maybe there's someone near you. Post a note on the bulletin board.

L: Will do. Thanks.

Willing to try anything, Leilani posted the note and received a reply later that morning. A member recommended Phyllis Leighton, a master hypnotherapist and regression counselor with an office about twenty miles west of Leilani's store.

Despite the early hour, Leilani called Phyllis and left a message on her voice mail. Not wanting to miss the return call, she took the cell phone along on her walk. She had almost completed her second mile when the phone rang.

"Hello?" she asked breathlessly.

"Please tell me you're out of breath for a good reason."

"Good morning, Neil. I'm walking. Can't stop yet. You talk."

"Just wanted to let you know you were right about the bicycle case. We lucked out a little. The house you described—perfectly, by the way—was only a few blocks away. It turned out to be nothing more than a case of a grade-schooler's revenge for being embarrassed in public. Adult tempers have been cooled. Thanks to you."

Leilani realized she had only heard the beginning and end of what he'd said. "Oh okay. That's good."

"What's going on, pal? You're not just out of breath."

She slowed her walk to cool-down mode. "I'm fine, really. I just have a dream I can't figure out and I can't let it go either."

"Wish I could help, but I'm in the dark when it comes to dreaming. Hah! Get it? In the dark?"

She groaned. "Thanks, but I've got a lead I'm going to follow."

"Whoa, girl. You better not mean you're doing any investigating—"

"No, no. I meant a lead to…oh never mind." She turned the corner that would take her back home. "Unfortunately, until I figure it out, I'm not sure how much help I'll be to you."

"Never worry about that. Oh I almost forgot, Edie wants you to come for dinner Thursday night. Are you free?"

"I'll make sure I am. See you then." At least she now had a confirmation that her gift of insight was still functioning properly, despite her bewilderment over the dream man.

No sooner was the call disconnected when the phone rang again. This time it was Phyllis Leighton. Leilani briefly explained why she had called while she went into her house and stripped off her sweaty clothes. "So my friend suggested I try looking at a past life."

"Regression therapy can certainly make a difference for a whole variety of problems, but there's no guarantee that one trip will be enough. It could take several sessions to get the information you're looking for. How much do you know about the process?"

"Just that it requires some form of hypnosis."

"Yes, but it's fairly mild, more like a guided meditation. The subject rarely goes into a deep sleep and usually remembers most of what he or she saw. A lot depends on a person's trust level with me, as well as her ability to let go of all circumstances of the present reality. It's not necessary, but it often helps when the subject is already familiar with meditating in one form or another. As a lucid dreamer, you shouldn't have any problem taking the leap easily."

"I hope you're right. Okay, I'd like to try. When could you fit me in?"

"I have an opening tomorrow evening at seven. It takes about two hours."

"Wonderful. I'll see you then. I've got an address but I'm not sure how to get there from here."

Phyllis gave her directions to her office. "If you have a few more minutes now, I'd like to hear a little more about this Lotus Circle you mentioned. It sounds like I'm missing a great networking opportunity."

Not having been as active as the other four members of the heart, Leilani gave her a little background and suggested she check out the website.

The rest of the day seemed to crawl by. She realized she was actually looking forward to going to sleep in hopes that she would have a dream that would resolve her dilemma before the appointment with Phyllis. There was something about the upcoming regression that made her stomach queasy. It felt a little like fear but not quite. She wasn't sure she wanted to know what had happened in a past life that would cause that feeling.

* * * * *

Swirls of gray fog drifting over his face...his eyes straining to pierce the haze...his mouth moves but no sound is heard.

Leilani woke in a cold sweat. Something was very, very wrong. It wasn't just the dream that was fading — it was the man. She was losing him!

The clock on her nightstand let her know it was still the middle of the night.

She tried to go back to sleep but couldn't let go of the sense that she was failing someone very important to her. After a half hour of tossing and turning, she got up, put on her painting clothes and resumed her ongoing project of refinishing the kitchen cabinets. As she scraped and sanded down the layers of old paint and varnish, she pretended she was peeling away the layers of fog that were preventing her from understanding the dream. Somehow, some way, she was going to get to the bottom of it, no matter how much, or what kind of, work it took.

Because of her interrupted sleep, she seemed to be in a fog herself all day. Finally, it was time to go see Phyllis Leighton.

Walking into the hypnotherapist's waiting room was a little like floating into one of her sweet dreams. The simple, uncluttered decor was all in soft pastels, a waterfall trickled in one corner and the framed prints on the walls included various winged creatures, like butterflies, hummingbirds and fairies. Soothing music was playing very quietly. Leilani was pretty sure if she sat down for a minute she'd fall fast asleep, but Phyllis came out of her office to greet her before she had a chance to test that thought.

"I hope traffic wasn't too bad for you," Phyllis said, directing her to enter the adjacent room.

"No worse than usual." Leilani thought Phyllis could have posed for one of the fairy pictures on the wall. Phyllis was a petite lady, nearly a head shorter than Leilani's five foot seven inches. Her eyes had a natural sparkle to them and her chin-length brown hair was a mass of frizzy curls. Leilani wondered if the unstyled hair actually hid little pointed ears.

Phyllis' inner office was quite different from the outer room. The colors were earthy and the furnishings were solid and well-stuffed. There were lots of pillows and throws and burning candles of various sizes and colors. It reminded Leilani of a turn-of-the century parlor.

"Is chamomile okay?" Phyllis asked, holding a pretty ceramic teapot with steam rising out of its spout.

Leilani's gaze moved from the inviting-looking couch to the small table set with flowers and a tea service for two. She had assumed she would be lying down for the regression. "Oh that would be fine, thank you." As she sat in a Queen Anne-styled chair, she noticed how cold the room was and gave both arms a quick rub.

Phyllis smiled and took the chair on the other side of the table. "I have to keep the air conditioning blasting in here. As soon as we begin the regression and call in our spirit guides, the temperature will rise noticeably. I have a feeling in your case, it's going to get downright hot. I read a little about lucid dreaming today, so that I might guide you into the past using references that should be familiar to you."

"Thank you. At this point, I'll take any help I can get. I tried to get more information myself last night."

"Oh?"

"Before I went to sleep, I asked a specific question about any possible past life with the man."

"And?"

"Nothing. Well, that's not entirely correct. It was the weakest dream I've had yet."

"Ah. I gather you think his problem, whatever it is he needs to be rescued from, has worsened. Okay, let me give you a small reassurance. As soon as we begin the regression, you will be strengthening the bond between you. Think of it like a lifeline. Last night it was just a thin thread, on the verge of being broken. After tonight, it should be stronger, maybe like a rope or even a chain that could be tugged on from either end."

"I sense a bond, that's for sure. But how is looking at a past life going to solve something in present time?"

Phyllis' eyes twinkled. "Because it's all connected. Something that occurs in one dimension can trickle across to affect circumstances in another dimension. You could compare it to how you see an event in your dreamtime and are able to do something about it in your conscious hours, ultimately causing a change or even preventing the event from happening."

"I guess I should have done some reading about reincarnation today."

"How about if I just give you my quickie version." She took a sip of her tea and encouraged Leilani to do the same. "Groups of souls tend to travel together through many lifetimes. Before entering a new life, they each have the ability to choose the role they will play, the theme of that lifetime and the lesson to be learned. Those individual choices determine which members of the group will encounter each other and in what capacity."

Leilani nodded her understanding of that much.

"You mentioned that your friend's card reading suggested that karma was involved. Karma comes into play in reincarnation when something occurs in one lifetime that is unresolved or needs to be balanced in a subsequent lifetime. Depending on the debt to be repaid or lesson to be learned, the resolution can be simple or incredibly complicated, especially if it has been repeated over many incarnations."

"In other words," Leilani concluded, "Rainy was right. The first step is to figure out what the karma is, and that can be done by looking at what happened when we were together before."

"Exactly. And similar to profiling a criminal, it could take more than one set of clues to determine a pattern. Also, two souls who are strongly connected may have had dozens, even hundreds of lives together, so it's important to focus on ones that have relevance to the question at hand. I'll guide you through that part, but it is very important that you let go of any preconceived notion of seeing a particular time period or place. Otherwise, you could end up somewhere when the two of you only had a passing acquaintance."

"That shouldn't be too hard for me. I've never given much thought to when or where I might have been before this life. And I'm fairly used to letting the Universe take me where I need to go in my dreamtime."

"Actually, you may find the process of regression simpler than dreaming to resolve problems. Few people are aware of their physical surroundings while they are dreaming. During the regression, you will still be vaguely aware of where your physical body is. It's almost as if the veil is lifted between your conscious and subconscious mind and both parts will be functioning simultaneously, yet separately."

"Um, I'm not sure I followed that."

Again, Phyllis' eyes sparkled with a light that came from within. "Your subconscious will be totally involved in another time and place. At the same time, your conscious will hear my voice and you'll be able to answer me without interfering with the sights or sounds of that other reality. As I mentioned before, you will remember a good deal of what your subconscious saw and heard, but as a backup, I always tape the session so you'll be able to review the details of your visit later. You may even hear tidbits that could confirm that the past life really occurred. Do you have any questions that I haven't covered?"

Leilani gave it a moment's thought then shrugged. "I can't think of anything else right now. Later may be a different story."

"All right then, let's get started." Phyllis asked her to take off her shoes and all metal jewelry that could possibly break the flow of magnetic energy through her body.

Leilani lay down on the couch, with her head and shoulders propped up on several fluffy pillows.

"Just relax," Phyllis said as she turned on a recording of various pleasant sounds of nature mixed with harp music. Next, she picked up a tuning fork and rod and held it above the top of Leilani's head. "Now, close your eyes and take a nice, slow breath, in through your nose and out through your mouth." She struck a high-pitched tone with the fork. "Continue to breathe gently, in and out." She struck a slightly lower tone above Leilani's eyes.

Leilani heard five more tones, each one a bit lower than the previous one, as Phyllis moved the fork downward over her body. Following each tone, Phyllis used different verbal instructions to take her into a more relaxed state, inch by inch helping her to let go of the restraints of her physical body, until she felt as though she was a free-floating spirit. She also noticed Phyllis' voice alter as she talked her through the relaxation process. It was gradual but, if Leilani didn't know better, she might have thought a completely different person was speaking now.

Then she felt the veil lift, and was in two places at the same time, exactly as Phyllis had said it would happen. She heard Phyllis' hypnotic voice guiding her to the foot of a bridge and realized that she had been standing there even before the words were spoken. On one level, she knew Phyllis was still speaking and that she was responding, but the other level was much stronger and drew her attention to the world she now found herself in. It had similarities to a dream but looked and felt much more detailed, more colorful, more *real*.

Phyllis asked for a protective spirit guide to take Leilani across the bridge. Two beings approached and each took one of her hands. One had wings, felt masculine and said his name was Micah. The other was Grandma. They assured Leilani that they would be with her through the whole journey, even when she couldn't see them. She was completely safe and could return to her physical body anytime she chose. Then they began to escort her across the bridge.

The bridge arched and vanished into a bluish-green mist, and she was told not to be afraid. From a distance, Phyllis' voice continued to guide her forward.

"You are entering the place between dimensions. If you look around, you will see glimpses of times and places you have experienced before. You are free to investigate any of them at another time. But this journey's purpose lies ahead. Focus on the face of the man you saw in

your dream. Focus on the words he said. And know that you are moving toward a time and place that is directly connected to the reason he is asking for your help now."

Leilani followed the instructions and the mist slowly dissipated, allowing her to see that she was descending the arched bridge.

"As you step off the bridge, you will no longer see your guides, but remember that they are always with you. You are completely protected. You have now reached your destination, a place where you and the man in your dreams were together…"

She had not felt the shift, yet it had already happened.

"Take a look around you."

She was lying in a four-poster canopied bed in an extremely frilly pink and white bedroom.

"Where are you?"

"In my bedroom," the little girl replied.

"And where is that bedroom?"

She giggled. "In my daddy's house, silly."

"What is your name?"

"Cassandra. But I like Cassie better."

"Well, hello, Cassie. Can you tell me how old you are?"

"Seven."

"That's practically all grown up. Imagine that you are looking in a mirror. Tell me what you look like."

This took a moment. "I have blonde hair and white skin, just like my mommy and daddy."

"Where is the house you all live in? Do you know the name of the country or town?"

"Saint Domingue."

"And what about the man from your dream? Does he live there too?"

She wrinkled her brow, searching for the answer. "Yes, but he's not in the house."

"Where does he live?"

"With the other slaves, of course."

"Cassie, what year is it?"

"Seventeen-ninety."

Chapter Three
Saint Domingue, 1790

"Wake up Miss Cassandra. I won't be havin' you sleep away dis beautiful day."

Slowly opening one eye, Cassie watched her nursemaid's large body waddle toward the windows. Sarah pulled back the heavy drapes and sunlight poured into the room, forcing Cassie to wipe the tears and sleep from her eyes. "Good morning, Sarah."

"Good mornin', Miss Ca— Oh my dear chile! Have you been cryin'? It was another one o' dem dreams, wasn't it?"

Cassie nodded.

"Don't let it upset you too much, chile. It was, after all, jus' a dream."

"I know. But what if it really happens like the other dreams?" Cassie bit on her lower lip to keep it from trembling.

Sarah sat down on the edge of the bed and took Cassie's hands. "Do ya wanna tell me about dis one?"

"It was about Joseph. There was a man who came to take him away, but I don't know where they were going."

"But dat don't sound like no reason to be cryin'. Maybe he was jus' goin' to see somebody."

"In the dream it seemed like he was leaving forever. It's just...he's my best friend. I...I don't want him to go away."

"Now, you know how it is. Y'all are gonna be eight next year. Joseph should've been put to work almost a year ago, but your papa decided to wait to put dat boy in dem fields. And since y'all gettin' older, it jus' ain't right for you both to still be playin' wit each other. I heard your folks talkin' da other day.

They said it be gettin' close to da time when you should be playin' wit dem other white boys and girls."

"But I don't want to play with them. I don't like them! I want to play with Joseph!" The tears started rolling down her cheeks and she began to angrily wipe them away.

Sarah pulled Cassie into her arms. "Settle down, chile, settle down. I know you don't want to hear it, but one day you will be da mistress of your own plantation jus' like your ma, and you can't be playin' wit da slave hands. It jus' ain't fittin' o' any white folk. Now let's get up and get you dressed. Your folks are downstairs waitin' to have breakfast with ya."

After breakfast Cassie went out in search of Joseph Whitely. She knew she would find him at their secret hiding spot down by the river. She skipped down her usual path along the row of one-room houses that served as the slaves' quarters lining her father's plantation. As usual, Harriet, adopted grandmother to all the slaves, was standing outside on her porch with a brood full of children. Cassie spotted her and skipped toward her.

"Good morning, Harriet," Cassie sang out.

"Well, good mornin', Miss Cassandra. I's sure mighty happy to see ya, chile. I've missed ya deez past few weeks."

"I've missed you too, Harriet."

"Jus' 'cause Joseph is gettin' big 'nough to take care o' his self don't mean ya can't still come by an' say hello to ol' Grandma Harriet. I's got everybody's babies to take care of but y'all grow up, don't ya?" Harriet's old, sun-withered face softened when one side of her mouth turned up in a smile. "'Nuff o' me. Where ya headed off to, baby?"

"Joseph and I are going to go dig up fishing worms today. Jean told him where we can find some extra big ones."

"Well in dat case come over here. I's got somethin' for ya." Harriet limped over to her rocking chair. As she sat down the chair groaned as if it were older than Harriet.

"Something for me?"

"O' course somethin' for *you*. Sarah done tol' me you've been doin' real good with your studies. Is dat true?"

"Uh-huh," Cassie said as she proudly rocked back and forth on her feet. "I have been studying really hard and Mr. Archer says I am very smart for my age. He says that if I keep it up I will know more than the older girls in town!"

"Oh, how excitin'! I knew you would do well." Harriet suddenly turned sober. "You jus' keep in mind dat der's a whole world o' opportunity out der for ya. Me, well...I's jus' born wit da wrong color skin. It ain't nothin' really. The Big Man upstairs, well...he's been watchin' over me since I's a baby. I's had a good life. But you...der ain't nothin' ya can't do. You hear me, chile?"

Cassie nodded. She had never seen Harriet so serious before. She watched Harriet reach into a basket on the floor and pull out a long thin piece of wood with engravings on it.

"I made dis for ya. It's to hold ya place in ya book when you be studyin'."

Cassie took the gift and quietly admired it. As her small fingers carefully traced the carvings she said, "This is beautiful, Harriet. Thank you so much. I'll take very good care of it."

"I know ya will, dear."

"But what do these markings mean?"

"Jus' an ol' woman's scratchins. Don't mean nothin'." Harriet leaned forward and winked. "But don't ya be surprised if ya have some special luck wit your lessons when ya use it." Reaching back into the basket, Harriet continued, "Oh, I almost forgot. I've got somethin' else for ya."

Cassie watched as Harriet pulled out a couple pieces of raw sugar cane. Licking her lips in anticipation, she replied, "For me?"

"Yep, but I's expect ya to be sharin' it wit Joseph, ya hear?"

Biting her bottom lip, she nodded as she held out her hand to take the valued treat. "Thank you again, Harriet."

"You're welcome, baby. Now go on and get outta here. And tell Joseph he needs to come an' pay a visit to an ol', lonely woman," Harriet said with a smile as she turned her attention back to the small herd of children.

"Bye Harriet!" Cassie shouted over her shoulder as she ran off to find Joseph. When she got to the river bank she spotted him sitting on the ground, staring into the water. Cassie realized he was so involved in his own thoughts that he didn't hear her approach until she stepped on a twig next to him.

A bit startled, Joseph said, "You didn't have to sneak up on me, Cass."

Laughing, Cassie said, "I didn't sneak up on you, silly. Why do you look so serious?" When he didn't answer, she sat down next to him on the ground. Following his gaze out over the water, she added softly, "I had the dream again. Sarah says that it isn't right for us to be playing with each other anymore." After a moment of lingering silence, Cassie turned toward Joseph only to see tears sliding quietly down his cheeks.

Joseph finally looked at her. "Da dreams are true, Cass. Dey be sendin' me away."

"What do you mean?" she asked with wide eyes.

Looking back at the water, Joseph continued, "Your pa sol' me to Masta Wyatt on da neighborin' plantation. Says he needs a strong back for dis season's sugar crop."

"But that can't be! Father wouldn't do that!"

"He did, Cass."

Cassie's eyes began welling up. "We need to do something! We can't let this happen!"

"I's jus' a slave, Cass. Ain't nothin' we can do," he said, still refusing to meet her gaze.

"But what about your mama?"

"She's stayin' here," he said with a sniffle. "But she says we'll be able to visit each other from time to time."

"But what about us?" No longer able to hold the tears back, she screamed at him. "*Look at me!* I won't have it! You're my best friend! I won't have you taken away from me!" Putting her face in her hands, she softly sobbed. "I won't have it. It's not fair."

He put his arm around her shoulder and the familiar, friendly gesture made her look up at him. "Don't you cry, Cass. At least I's be nearby. We can sneak away to see each other whenever we git da chance."

Cassie wiped her nose with the back of her hand. "Promise?"

"Promise."

As always, they sealed their promise with a secret handshake.

The next morning, Cassie watched from her bedroom window as Mister Wyatt took Joseph away in his wagon. When her best friend glanced up and saw her, she placed her palm on the pane of glass as another tear fell down her cheek.

* * * * *

"Time to git up, Miss Cassandra. Breakfast is long gone an' here you is, still in your bed sleepin'. It's a shameful thing to waste da day like dis."

"Just let me sleep a few more minutes, Sarah. I won't tell. Please."

"It's been weeks o' dis laziness. Ah, but I know better den dat, chile. Don't ya think for a minute dat I's got me no brain in my head to think wit. I know ya been sneakin' 'round after everyone's sleepin'. You ain't got no sense at all, chile. What would your folks say if dey knew der daughter was sneakin' around at night? And to see a nigga? You ain't got no sense at all. No sense."

Cassie watched as Sarah paced her room. She was just woken from a bad dream, but it was the same one she'd had for the past several nights. "How did you know?"

"I's been wit ya since you was a baby, chile. I know you better dan ya know yourself. But what *you* don't know is dat ya gonna git dat boy in a whole world full o' trouble."

Cassie sat straight up in bed. She couldn't believe what Sarah just said. Her bad dreams had been about Joseph being in trouble and hurt. "What did you say? What kind of trouble is Joseph going to get in?"

"Dat Masta Wyatt ain't da nice man your papa is. He don't put up with no nigga o' his doin' whatever dey please. You need to end your friendship wit dat boy before ya get him whipped."

"Whipped?"

"Dats right, *whipped*. Da two o' ya live in different worlds and it's best time you be realizin' dat."

* * * * *

Cassie waited until she was certain everyone in the house was asleep that night before climbing out her window and down the tree that had aided her so well in the past. Her feet touched the dewy grass and she quietly ran to meet Joseph at the river. Halfway there she felt a few sprinkles of rain but knew she couldn't turn back. She needed to tell Joseph about her dreams. The rain only made her move faster to get to him.

When she reached the river, she called out, "Are you here? Joseph? Where are you?" *Where is he? He's always here before me.* Not wanting to leave without warning him, Cassie sat on the ground and hugged her knees to her chest. As the drizzle turned into a downpour, it felt as though the sky was crying for her friend.

By the time the rain was finally letting up, Cassie was shivering from head to toe. She wasn't sure what happened to Joseph. He had always shown up before when they had plans to meet. Either way, she needed to get home before anyone knew she was missing.

After climbing back up into her room she dropped her soaked clothes in a heap on the floor, put on her pajamas and crawled into bed. She knew she would get an earful from Sarah in the morning, but she was too tired and cold to care at the moment.

* * * * *

"Cassandra, it's about time you made it down to breakfast. We have some things we need to discuss with you," her father said in a serious tone.

She wasn't sure what was going on but knew by looking at her parents that she was in trouble.

Her father continued. "Would you care to explain why Sarah found your clothes soaking wet in a pile on your floor this morning?"

Before Cassie could come up with a plausible excuse, her mother interjected, "There is no need to try to think up a lie for us, Cassandra. Sarah also informed us that you have been sneaking around at all hours of the night to see Joseph. This is *not* something we will tolerate. You have reached an age where it is no longer appropriate for a young lady of your standing to be spending time with a slave hand. Do you understand?"

Cassie folded her hands in her lap and lowered her head. "Yes ma'am."

"I want to be sure you are understanding us, Cassandra," her father added. "You are not to see this boy again. *Ever.* Are we making ourselves clear?"

"Yes, sir."

Breakfast continued quietly. As soon as she was dismissed, she ignored her parents' warnings and went out in search of Joseph. Cassie was worried about why he didn't show up last night. She knew the first place to look for him would be down by the river. When Cassie reached the water she was filled with relief to see Joseph standing there, skipping rocks over the river's clear surface. She ran to him and, as he turned to her, she threw her arms around him and hugged with all her might.

"Where were you last night? I waited for hours in the rain and you never showed. I was really, really worried. I've been having these dreams—" Cassie stepped back as she felt him cringe from her hug. "What's wrong, Joseph?"

"Nothin'."

When he turned again toward the water Cassie noticed some blood on the back of his shirt that had not been there before. "Oh my goodness, Joseph, you're *bleeding*!"

As she reached out her hand to touch the blood, he stepped away from her. "Please Cass, leave it alone," he said, throwing another rock.

"I will, as soon as you tell me what's going on. I've been having terrible dreams about you being hurt and I came here last night to warn you about them, but you weren't here."

"I don't know how ya do it, but dem dreams always come true, don't dey?"

Rather than answer, Cassie asked, "What happened?"

"I's got me in some trouble yesterday, Cass. It warn't no big deal or nothin'. I was workin' for most da mornin' cleanin' Masta Wyatt's tools but I was usin' da wrong oil. When da boss came over to yell at me dis man stepped in his way to try an' stop him. He told him dat I's jus' a youngin' an' don't know no better. Den da boss took him an' started to whip him for interferin'. When I tried to stop it, he gave me a few lashes o' my own. He said it's for me to remember my place and to remind me dat I's jus' a slave."

Cassie was horrified. She had never seen such violence on her father's plantation but had heard that it happened elsewhere on the island.

"Don't worry, Cass. I's all right. Besides, it turns out dat da man who tried to help me is my Uncle Daniel. My mama done tol' me 'bout him 'fore I left, but I jus' met him yesterday. He took care o' my cuts and said he's gonna teach me how to get by."

"Are you sure you're all right?" Cassie asked timidly.

"I swear, I'm fine. It ain't dat bad."

When Cassie kept frowning at him, Joseph told her about the other boys he lived with and some of the funny things they had done. By the time he told her his third story she was laughing.

"I miss playing with you, Joseph. We've always had so much fun together. It isn't the same with the other boys and girls. My parents told me this morning that I was no longer allowed to play with you." Cassie picked up a smooth rock and threw it over the water.

"You're my best friend, Cass. Always have been and always will be. There's nobody else I'd rather play with or talk to."

"Yeah, I know what you mean, Joseph." Cassie was quiet for a moment then brightened up when an idea came to her. "I know. I say we make a pact. From this moment on, no matter what happens, we will stay best friends forever and ever, until the end of the world." Cassie stuck out her hand for their secret handshake.

"I can't imagine anybody else bein' my best friend," Joseph replied as he shook her hand.

To his great shock, Cassie leaned over and sealed their promise with a kiss on his cheek.

True to their vow, they found ways to stay in touch secretly for nearly a year.

* * * * *

July, 1791

Cassie lay on the ground staring up at the branches that filtered the sun's rays. "I think that our spot is the only place on the whole island that doesn't feel like an oven." The sound of the water drifting lazily by added to her contentment.

"I think you be right 'bout dat, but don't try an' change da subject." Joseph took his place on the ground next to her. "We already know when ya have dreams like dis, dey often come true. Now try an' think real hard. What else happens...an' don't ya tell me ya don't know. You've had dis dream for the past two weeks straight."

"I've already told you everything I can think of. All I know is that it seems like I'm in terrible, terrible danger and you're trying to get to me to help. I don't know why, but for some reason, you can't. And then, like I've said before, everything goes dark and I wake up terrified and shaking."

"I don't know what all dis means, but give your word you'll try to be careful 'til we can figure it out."

"Trust me, I will. It scares me just talking about it," Cassie said with a shiver. "Anyway, it's getting late and your free time is almost up. I don't want you to get into any trouble. I'll see you next Sunday?"

"Yep, next Sunday."

The walk back to the plantation in the tropical heat nearly took all of Joseph's energy away. Because Sunday was the one day the Wyatts allowed their slaves free time, there were few people outside. When he reached the slaves' quarters that outlined the property, he sat down in the shade on the porch of his uncle's one-room house. He heard someone talking to his uncle inside, so he figured he would rest there until the stranger left.

As he closed his eyes, he felt the sweat trickling down his brow. He was curious as to what they were whispering about inside, but long ago his uncle had taught him the value of minding his own business, so he went back to concentrating on cooling down. It wasn't until he heard his uncle raise his voice that his curiosity got the best of him. Scooting closer to the window, he could just make out what they were saying.

"But da French were more dan successful! Don't you understand?" the stranger exclaimed.

"But dat be two years ago."

"Exactly! Two years an' da merchant ships still be bringin' us news of der success."

"Dey'd crush us immediately. Like bugs!"

"Dat be your fear talkin', Daniel! You don't think da French were scared? Dey were frightened to death, but dey chose not to live like dat no more, repressed an' in fear. Fear o' dying at da hands of someone wit power for no reason at all. Fear o' dyin' 'cause there be no food in der stomachs. Fear o' watchin' der babies die 'cause dey have no more food to give dem. An' look what happened. Da people wit da power were brought down along wit da *king an' queen*. I am tired o' watchin' our people die. It is cheaper for da whites to buy new slaves dan to feed us and keep us healthy an' dat is what dey choose to do! Let us die for der profit's sake!"

Daniel cut him off before he could continue his passionate speech. "I know all dis already, but do ya really think der's somethin' we can do about it?"

"Don't ya see? *Dey fear us!* It is in our numbers dat we are strongest. Because o' dis, dey try an' keep us inferior. Dey refuse to educate us for fear we will learn da truth of how *we* are da ones who wield da power over *dem*. Don't you think it be time we both stop hiding da fact dat we can read an' write? We were taught in secret, but don't ya want to pass our knowledge on to others openly without da fear o' bein' killed for it? I am tired of pretendin' to be a foolish man, no better dan an ass, because it makes dem feel safe. It is time we lead our people out o' da darkness dey be shut up in."

"You don't think I care about our people?" Daniel countered. "It grieves me every day to watch what goes on here on dis island. Da masters and mistresses here talk of God and holiness but dey are da worst kind o' sinners. Da only thing dat gets me through da days is knowing dat when I get to the Lord's home, deez sinful people will not be welcomed der an' I will finally be at peace."

"Daniel, I need to know if we can count on ya. Toussaint be a great man wit da visions of a future filled wit da freedom we crave for our people. We outnumber dem by da thousands. We jus' need da courage to stand up an' fight. Because without freedom der be no life worth livin'."

After a moment's hesitation, Daniel replied, "I know you be right. You can count on me."

"Good. I knew I could. I will meet wit you soon and tell ya when we strike. Now, it's time I must be goin'. Dis meetin' never happened, understood?"

"Yes."

Joseph heard footsteps heading toward the door and he slid off the porch, around the side of the house and out of sight. He waited until he saw the stranger disappear down the path before he came out from hiding. When he walked through the door his uncle looked surprised to see him.

"Joseph, I didn't think you'd be back so soon. How was your—"

"Who was dat man, Uncle Daniel?"

"What? Oh, um…he's an ol' friend."

"What he be doin' here?" When it looked like his uncle was thinking up a story to tell him, Joseph demanded, "Don't lie to me, Uncle Daniel. I ain't a baby no more. An' I ain't stupid either. I heard some of what you were talkin' 'bout. Now explain."

"You're right, Joseph. You ain't no baby no more." Daniel paused a moment then sighed. "Our people have been stolen from our homeland an' brought here to dis island for over one hundred an' sixty years. You be lucky nuff to be born here an' not see what I seen. Babies snatched away from der mother's breast an' left in da sun to die because dey were jus' babies an' no work could come outta dem. But change be comin'. Der be a great number who are ready to fight for what be belongin' to us by birth. A gift from God dat no man has da right to take away."

"What's dat?"

"Freedom, Joseph. And the white masters won't be givin' it to us without a battle."

"Dis sound real scary, Uncle Daniel. I's don't like it none."

"Everythin' will be okay. You are jus' gonna have to trust me, Joseph. Now what we jus' talked about can never leave dis room, ya hear? If anyone were to find out 'bout dis, dey'd come an' kill us all. Do ya understand what I be tellin' ya, boy?"

Joseph nodded his head nervously. "Y-yes, Uncle Daniel. I don't wanna see no one gettin' hurt cause o' me."

"I know ya don't, Joseph. But when I say nobody can know, I mean *nobody*."

Joseph wondered if his uncle knew about his secret visits with Cassie. "I promise. When all dis gonna be happenin'?"

"I'll let ya know when da time has come."

* * * * *

August, 1791

"Joseph. Joseph, wake up."

"Huh? Uncle Daniel, what's goin' on? Is it mornin' already?" Joseph asked his uncle sleepily.

"No, Joseph. It ain't da mornin', but it be time for action. Everyone is gatherin' an' it won't be safe for ya to stay here by yourself."

This got Joseph's attention. It had been a few weeks since his uncle had told him about the plans but he had felt the anticipation rising around him since then. "All right, I'm ready."

"We are takin' control of dis here island…*tonight*. Don't be scared, Joseph. I can see da panic in your eyes, but after tonight, we'll all be free."

Joseph nodded apprehensively, but before he could say anything, his uncle pulled him outside and into a large crowd of slaves, all moving silently toward the master's house. He wasn't sure what they were going to do or how they were going to do it, but his questions were soon answered.

When the crowd arrived at the steps leading to the Wyatts' home, the front door slowly creaked open, disturbing the quiet tension. One of the Wyatts' female house slaves stepped into the moonlight.

Joseph heard the man at the front of the gathering whisper, "Good girl. Now get outta here an' hide. And don't ya come out 'til mornin'…no matter what."

She quickly ran off as the sea of slaves noiselessly flowed into the house.

The Wyatts' son was in the kitchen drinking a glass of milk when one of the slaves crept up behind him and pulled out a dagger. He grabbed the boy's hair and, in one fluid movement, slashed his throat. The glass of milk crashed to the floor, shattering the silence. Joseph felt bile rise as he watched blood instantly gush out of the boy's throat. Frozen with shock, Joseph had to be dragged out of the room by his uncle to keep up with the others.

"What the hell is going on here?" Master Wyatt demanded from the top of the stairs. It was clear that he did not know whether to be angry, shocked or terrified at the sight of all the slaves in his house.

The leader of the pack confidently climbed the stairs toward the master. "We have come to pay respect to our masta." When he reached the landing, the slave revealed his dagger, still dripping with the boy's blood. Before Wyatt could run, he grabbed the back of the white man's nightshirt and asked, "Where ya think ya goin'," he slashed the man's throat, "*Masta*?"

As Wyatt crumpled to the floor, the leader turned to the crowd and coldly said, "Finish it."

Excited shouts rose up from the mob as they rushed up the stairs in search of the rest of the family. They found Wyatt's wife, sister and daughter in a room, huddled together crying. One slave aimed a rifle at the little girl and shot her in the head. Both women let out piercing screams, but it did nothing to stop their attackers. Two machete- wielding slaves swiftly moved in on the women and silenced them.

Joseph stared in horror as they continued to hack at the bodies long after they were dead. His uncle grabbed his arm and dragged him downstairs and outside, while others began setting fires. From the front lawn, the slaves cheered as the house became engulfed in flames. Already feeling sick from what he had just witnessed, the putrid smoke caused Joseph's stomach to revolt.

By the time he stopped vomiting, another, even larger group of slaves had joined them. To Joseph, they all seemed to have crazed looks in their eyes. He wanted to go home. He wanted no part of what they were doing. But the mob was on the move again, and he was being carried along regardless of what he wanted or didn't want.

When they reached their next target, Joseph closed his eyes rather than watch another family being massacred, but he could not shut out their cries. When they left the second house, he could hear screams coming from all over the area. Other mobs were moving through different parts of the island, killing and destroying everything white that stood in their paths. As more and more homes were set on fire, the night sky became filled with thick smoke.

Suddenly, Joseph realized that the path Uncle Daniel was pulling him along was heading straight for Cassie's house.

Dis must be what Cass has been dreamin' 'bout! Joseph thought. He dug his heels into the ground and begged, "Please, Uncle Daniel, leave deez people alone. Dey be good people. Dey were always kind to me. Please don't hurt dem." His pleading got him nowhere. His uncle just kept hauling him along, as though he couldn't hear him.

As the mob approached Cassie's property, they began to run. Daniel's grip on Joseph was broken and they were separated in an instant. Joseph's only thought was to cut away from the crowd and go in the side entrance of the house in time to warn Cassie. But there were so many of them and he was so small.

Just as he started to move in a different direction, someone pushed him and he fell. Before he could get to his feet, he was trampled by the hoard behind him. Searing pain shot through his body as he felt his leg bone snap. He tried to get up but it was hopeless. He only managed to pull himself a few feet along the ground when he heard the first scream come from Cassie's house. Desperately he crawled forward, ignoring the pain. Before he ever neared the side door, the screams had stopped, the fires had been set and the entire second story of the house collapsed.

He was too late to save her.

Chapter Four

An enormous crowd of people...laughing, shouting...loud music...celebration...a parade...colorful costumes...everyone is having such a good time...

Leilani awoke slowly, despite the fact that she had gone to bed earlier than usual and it was now an hour later than she normally started her day. Rather than refreshing her, the extra sleep seemed to have left her even groggier than she'd been yesterday.

It was impossible to tell immediately where the regression session ended and the dreams began. It had been an active dream night. Unfortunately, most of it seemed to involve processing the information gleaned from her time with Phyllis. All night long she watched reruns of the short life she had experienced as Cassandra.

The only thing new on her notepad had to do with some sort of celebration. She transcribed her notes into her journal and staggered to the kitchen. She needed coffee, lots and lots of coffee.

As the caffeine cleared the cobwebs from her brain, she began to recall the events of the evening before. It had felt as though she had been on her "trip" for about ten minutes, but it had actually been nearly two hours.

Phyllis had talked Leilani back into her body and made her drink a glass of water to ground her. She had kept her from driving for another half hour by going over the details of the regression. Even still, Leilani was fairly sure that her car had found its way home on autopilot.

Despite Phyllis warning her not to have any preconceived notions, she had assumed she would see the man looking like he did in her dream. Yet, his appearance as the young slave had not kept her from recognizing him the moment she saw him in the regression.

What was really bothering her this morning was disappointment. She had hoped the session would result in her knowing who the man was and how she could help. Instead, she had seen a lifetime in which she was brutally murdered and he had not been able to save her, even though Cassandra had given him a warning. The night before, the man seemed to be fading. Last night, he didn't show up at all. Had she failed him? Did that mean she had failed to save him as he had failed to save her?

On the other hand, Phyllis had told her that a good regression session could strengthen the bond. Perhaps just the act of reviewing a past life they shared was enough to pull him out of trouble. Perhaps the happy dream scene was letting her know she had done it. The people certainly appeared to be celebrating. It also felt like she was seeing a future event, which should have given her hope of a positive outcome. The fact that she did not feel any sense of relief just added to her bewilderment.

Her attempts at analysis were interrupted when her gaze fell on an article in the paper's business section. A client had asked her for some career advice a few months ago and she must have heeded it. She was just promoted to vice president of the company she had been thinking of leaving. She needed that sort of news today. She needed a reminder that she helped a lot of people with her gift. Leilani smiled as she made a notation in her journal.

By the time she got back from her walk, however, she was back to fretting over the dream man. Not knowing what else to do, she decided to listen to the tape of her regression session. For the next two hours she sat with her eyes closed and watched the movie in her head while her hand rapidly scribbled notes.

She was stunned to hear herself speaking in the slightly accented little girl's voice. She was even more surprised that the end of that life was seen from the slave boy's viewpoint. She knew she had been killed only because he knew about it. She had not personally relived the experience. What was most intriguing, however, was that she was certain she had no knowledge of a place called Saint Domingue or a slave rebellion that occurred in 1791.

A few minutes later, she was surfing the web to confirm or negate what she had seen in her session with Phyllis.

It didn't take long to learn that Saint Domingue was the name of the island now known as Haiti and that the slave population had indeed massacred a great number of the wealthy, white plantation owners in 1791. There were other confirming details as well, like the name Toussaint. The leader of the rebellion was a slave who had been treated kindly by his white owners, even allowing him to be educated, though such leniency could have been punishable by death. Toussaint had taken that education and shared it with other slaves in secret. Inspired by the success of the French revolution, he built an army of slaves, many of whom had good reason to hate their white masters.

All of it had happened exactly as she had seen and heard. She had been one of the wealthy white children who were mindlessly butchered alongside their parents. Knowing that, however, was not much help in explaining the dreams of the dark-haired man, even if he used to be a childhood friend named Joseph Whitely.

Suddenly she realized what time it was and jumped up from her chair. Because of her invitation to have dinner with Neil's family that night, Tillie had agreed to exchange shifts with her, but she had forgotten all about both things.

That set the pace for the rest of Leilani's day. She was late opening the store, late heading home and late arriving at the Fosters' house.

As she stepped out of her car in their driveway, she heard the sounds of splashing and youthful squeals of delight rising from the backyard and didn't bother to try the front door. Neil was in the pool with seven-year-old Deke and nine-year-old Daisy.

"Hey, everybody," he shouted. "Look who's here!"

The kids acknowledged her arrival with quick waves then went right back to trying to dunk their father.

"You look lovely, as usual," Edie said as she came out the back door carrying a tray of shish kebabs. "Hope you're hungry."

"Famished. I think I forgot to eat lunch today."

Edie shook her head with a chuckle and patted her hip. "I wish I could forget to eat a meal or two! I know you always turn me down, but I just whipped up a batch of margaritas…"

"Thanks, but no thanks. I'm not kidding about not being able to handle liquor. One glass of wine knocks me right out. I'm just one of those people who has zero tolerance for anything narcotic. Can I help with anything?"

"Sure. The salads and relish tray are in the fridge. You can bring them out while I put these on the grill."

Leilani noted that the picnic table inside the screened-in patio was already set. They obviously had everything ready and were just waiting for her. "I'm so sorry I'm late. I just couldn't seem to catch up today."

"Neil said you were having a problem. Anything I can help with?"

"Feeding me will be plenty."

"Everybody out of the pool!" Edie shouted loudly enough for the neighbors to hear, though her raucous family managed not to notice until she threatened to give their portions to the dog.

"I did have a very interesting experience last night. I think you might—"

"Hello?" a male voice called from the other side of the fence.

Edie hurried to open the gate. "I'm so sorry! I didn't think to tell you we'd be in the backyard." When she came back into the patio area, she had a man in tow.

"Leilani, this is Calvin Trees, a new friend of mine from church. He's just moved here from Akron and he has the most incredible voice."

He stepped around his spokesperson and held out his hand. "Hello. It's a pleasure."

As she accepted his handshake, Leilani felt the smooth, baritone voice vibrate from his hand into hers. He was tall enough, lean enough and nice looking enough to impress the average single girl. And he had a voice that would surely sound even sexier in the dark. He was also openly staring at her with the blatant relief of a man who had prepared himself for the worst and was thrilled that she was close to a wish come true. Being tricked into yet another setup, however, kept her from jumping for joy. She smiled and reclaimed her hand. "Welcome to Melbourne, Calvin."

"Cal, please. I hope you don't mind my asking, but Edie didn't tell me too much about you. Are you from Hawaii or one of the other Polynesian islands?"

Before she could answer, Neil and the kids joined them, wrapped in towels. He glanced at Leilani and tried to send her a *this-wasn't-my-idea* look. "Hey, Cal. Nice to see you again."

Leilani purposely avoided sitting next to Cal, only to end up with him directly across from her. For a few minutes, everyone's attention was focused on filling up their plates, but all too soon the interview started again.

"I apologize if I seem to be staring," he said nicely, in that deliciously deep voice, "but once upon a time I thought about majoring in anthropology and I really am curious about your heritage."

Leilani swallowed the bite of grilled mushroom in her mouth and ordered herself to be cordial. After all, this wasn't his fault. "My mother was Hawaiian-born. My father, however, is an all-American stew-pot, a little bit of a lot of different ethnic origins."

Cal's mouth tilted up on one side. "That explains the beautiful cheekbones and black hair. But for those incredible blue eyes and fair skin to come out, there must have been some strong German or Scandinavian genes. Am I right?"

"Yep."

The conversation came to an abrupt halt with that reply and Edie jumped in. "Cal is a professor of microbiology. He tried to explain what that is, but I'm afraid it's over my head. Maybe Neil or Leilani would understand better."

Cal hesitated for a second and Leilani couldn't tell if he was embarrassed about being put on the spot or just feigning modesty. Either way, as he launched into an explanation of what he considered an important topic, Deke and Daisy saved everyone by starting an elbow fight and Edie had to split them up. Neil grabbed the conversational ball and redirected it toward what the kids were studying in school.

For that act of kindness, Leilani almost forgave Neil for the setup. The fact was, she had asked him not to try fixing her up with any more of his cop friends. It hadn't occurred to her that she needed to threaten Edie about *her* friends also. She knew they meant well. Married people always seemed to think that everyone should be married. Just as parents tended to believe that everyone should experience parenthood, regardless of the trials and tribulations that go along with either of those choices.

Leilani had nothing against marriage. It was just that, after a series of hurtful experiences in the dating ring, she simply knew she was better off single. She stole a glance at Cal. When she was still in her twenties, she would have been interested in seeing more of him. But she had learned the hard way that, no matter how much potential a relationship seemed to have at the beginning, it would soon fall apart and someone would get hurt. And, almost always, it was her fault.

She was rigidly set in her ways and routines. No man she'd met had been able to understand why she couldn't just skip this part of her day or that to spend time with him. No one had ever comprehended that it was her rigid routines that kept her two worlds in balance.

She could not sleep in the same bed, or even the same room, with another person. In fact, her home was rather small, so someone moving about in the living room could be disruptive. Her dreamtime was affected by the physical reality her body was in, even if she was asleep. What made matters worse was that the other person was unable to rest with her frequent sleep-talking and partial waking to take notes. Making love to a man then asking him to leave her house was not conducive to a long-term relationship.

It had been so long since she'd had sex that her body didn't even ache for it any more. It used to be that she would wish for a sexy, passionate man whose career required him to be out of town more than he was in. Someone whom she could occasionally date and have sex with, and they would both be happy with the arrangement. Of course, there had been offers from married men who were more than willing to have a hit-and-run relationship, as long as it could be kept secret. That was not an acceptable option.

The best scenario she could imagine would be to find a man with his own special gifts or challenges that she needed to be understanding about. The only kind of man she could have in her life full-time was one who needed compromise as much as she did and, so far, no such man had dropped out of the sky.

Without asking any leading questions, Leilani guessed that Cal would fall into the category of men who ran from her for another reason. Edie said she met him at church, plus he taught science. Right there, the odds were pretty low that he would understand her spiritual outlook. Even without the church-going or scientific connections, Leilani had encountered a lot of men who found her "too spooky" to date more than once.

Years ago she had determined that, rather than hide her gifts or spirituality, or lower her personal standards, she would simply give up on intimate relationships with men.

"Will you be free Sunday afternoon?" Cal asked her.

Up to that moment, she had managed to move her gaze around the group and smile when they did, without actually participating in the conversation. Apparently, she had missed something important. She took a sip of iced tea as though needing to wash down another bite before answering.

"I've heard these monthly socials at the church are a lot of fun. Couldn't Tillie cover for you for a few hours?" Edie asked.

"Actually," Neil interceded quickly, "I already claimed Lani's Sunday afternoon. I thought I mentioned it to you. It's the only time both of us have to review a new stack of cold cases."

Edie cocked an eyebrow at him. "No, I don't think you mentioned that."

"I thought you owned a store," Cal said, not noticing the exchange. "I didn't realize you also worked for the police department."

"She's a psychic," Daisy declared in a matter-of-fact tone.

Cal started to laugh, then, noticing the tense reaction of the adults, realized the child's statement was not a joke. "Oh. Really? I, uh, I don't think I've ever met a psychic. I mean I've seen movies, and there're quite a few shows on television now, but I haven't ever, I mean…what exactly do you do for the police department?"

Leilani stopped herself from sighing. The poor man had already showed his thoughts in his eyes. In a heartbeat he had gone from intense attraction to scientific curiosity to fear. Her grandmother had taught her how to live with her gifts and deal kindly with people who felt negatively about them. She smiled. "It's nothing really. Every once in a while I get lucky, that's all."

Daisy was about to say something else, but Edie stopped her before she had time to light another firecracker.

Immediately after the table was cleared and the children were sent inside to watch a movie, Cal said the appropriate "thank you" and "nice to meet you" and left the spooky woman behind.

"I'm sorry, Lani," Edie said sincerely. "I really thought he—"

"Don't. Please. I'm not upset. But this *has* to be the last time. Invite me over to visit with the four of you anytime, but I need you to respect my wishes about no setups from now on. Okay?"

"We promise," Neil said for both of them. "How about coming in for coffee and another piece of cake, maybe watch the movie with the kids?"

"Thanks, but I need to go." After hugs all around, she headed home.

She really wasn't upset with them. She was just tired. All she needed was a good night's sleep and she'd be back to normal in the morning.

Perhaps because she was so tired, she had a hard time controlling her thoughts. This evening had reminded her of how she used to wish for a loving male partner and why she no longer held any expectations in that area. Tonight, that memory made her feel sad and she rarely let that emotion take hold. To be honest, however, she couldn't blame it all on this one night. Those thoughts had started to reawaken shortly after she had learned about The Lotus Circle.

Until three months ago, she had been content with the probability that she would never marry or have children. Watching Neil's family in action always gave her a wonderfully warm feeling. And she enjoyed playing with her little neighbors Nina and Maddy. And she understood how many women needed children to feel fulfilled. But she had never heard her own biological clock ticking or felt a strong desire to get pregnant.

Then she learned that she was part of a group of women sworn to pass on their gifts and knowledge to their daughters, sworn to pass the torch and spread the light around the world. No one had pushed her. The sense of obligation and responsibility had risen within her, as though on some level she had always known there was something important she had promised to do in this lifetime. Her mother and grandmother were gone. She had no sisters or female cousins. If she didn't have a daughter, her inheritance, her gifts and her family's maternal line would die with her.

Until three months ago, she had not known that what was missing in her life was a little girl of her own.

Chapter Five

The man is distinct...his whole upper body now visible...his expression grim, hopeless...he seems frozen in position...is he tied? Restrained? Locked in? The room around him is stark, shabby, gray...the only color is on a calendar hanging behind his head...a date, March 10, circled in red...the circle begins to bleed...dark crimson blood dripping down the calendar onto the man's shoulder...

Again, Leilani woke up gasping for breath. Although she was quite sure the images would not fade anytime soon, she quickly scribbled everything she just saw. Her mind struggled to assimilate what the dream meant. The man was still alive and still in some sort of trouble. He could be a kidnap victim or prisoner of war. One thing was very certain. A deadline had now been set and blood would flow, including his, if someone didn't soon figure out where he was.

The date, March 10, was less than three weeks away. The date itself meant nothing to her, yet in the dream she felt that it had relevance to the whole mystery. Fear had flooded every cell of her body when she saw the date dripping blood. She had to work hard to let go of that sense of fear now that she was awake. A part of her mind was shouting that something terrible was going to happen and she needed to act urgently. She could call Neil, but what would she tell him? Something bad is going to happen somewhere, to some unknown man, on March 10?

She closed her eyes and tried to scan the room again, but the dream images had already begun to fade.

The good news was that the images had been completely clear when she was dreaming and she now saw more of the man and his surroundings than she had before. It definitely looked like Phyllis was right about the bond between them strengthening after the regression. With no other ideas, she decided to request another session with Phyllis as soon as possible.

No sooner did she have that thought than her body relaxed, confirming that it was the right decision. A few minutes later, she was able to go back to sleep.

When she woke up several hours later, she felt so much better that she immediately called Phyllis.

"Good morning, Leilani. Are you all right?"

"I'm sorry to call you so early, but the dream has become more urgent and I'm hoping you can squeeze me in for another session."

"Well, normally I like to leave at least two weeks of processing time in between sessions."

"In two weeks the man could be dead."

"In that case, I'll see you this evening."

Next she called Tillie to make sure she could work the closing shift again. She had to promise a full explanation when they had tea later, but as usual, she was able to count on Tillie.

Leilani was at the store for over an hour before the first customer came in. Except for Saturdays, which were always busy, and Sundays, when the store was closed, there never seemed to be a particular pattern to the traffic flow in the store. Thankfully, this looked like it was going to be one of the quiet days when she was able to clean and straighten up.

She was rearranging books in a far corner of the room when she suddenly felt an uncomfortable sensation in her stomach and quickly turned to see what, or who, had caused it. She wasn't sure how she had missed the sound of the little bell on the front door, but someone had entered.

As she walked around the end of a display shelf, she nearly bumped into Randy Krupp, coming from the other direction.

"Oh! Hello again. I'm sorry, I didn't hear the bell."

He did the same nervous shifting he had done before. "I, uh, I…" He cleared his throat and looked into her eyes for a split second before focusing on a tiny wooden bear on the shelf. "This is cute. It's my nephew's first birthday and I don't know what to buy him."

She struggled to control a need to move as far away from him as possible. "Well, this could be the beginning of a collection for the child's room, either carved wooden animals or bears of all sorts. You know, something you could add to on each birthday."

He grinned from ear to ear and was able to meet her gaze directly for several seconds. "That is a *wonderful* idea. Thank you."

"I'll get you the box from the back." There was a box for the bear under the counter, but she felt desperate to get away from him. By the time she returned and took the box up to the cash register, she had gathered her composure again. "Was there anything else I could help you with today?"

She regretted asking the question the instant she saw the flush rise on his cheeks.

"I, uh, I was wondering if, um…" He looked as though he was having trouble breathing.

"Mr. Krupp? Are you all right?"

He held up a finger then fumbled in his pants pocket for a moment. As soon as she saw him bring an inhaler up to his mouth, she relaxed. She wasn't going to have to call 9-1-1 after all. Whatever he was about to ask her had gotten him so nervous, it triggered an asthma attack.

Who was she kidding? She knew very well what he was about to ask, at least in a general sense. Mr. Krupp had been about to ask her out. That in itself was not an unusual problem. She would have used one of her standard excuses for turning men down. What bothered her was the uncomfortable feeling she got when he was nearby. He had done nothing to warrant that reaction and yet her body was telling her he was dangerous — and she always trusted her body's messages.

* * * * *

Leilani arrived for her second regression session fifteen minutes early, but Phyllis was ready for her.

As before, Phyllis served tea, but this time Leilani did most of the talking.

When she was up to date, Phyllis noted, "Considering how much work you do out of your physical body, I'm not at all surprised at how quickly you processed the information and strengthened the visual you were getting. Tonight's journey is going to start the same way, but as you cross the bridge, I want you to mentally add that you are looking for another lifetime, when the two of you were together as adults, *not* the one in Saint Domingue, when the two of you were children. We want to make sure we get new information so that we can compare and, hopefully, find some common element."

This time, Leilani was walking across the bridge with her guides before Phyllis struck the third tone with her fork.

Chapter Six
Salem Village, Massachusetts
Late April, 1692

"Now, Hannah Falkner, you *need* to speak of it, at least with us," Ruth proclaimed in the voice that let everyone know she was the authority on all goings-on in Salem Village. "You know very well that there is already a rumor of it." The other two matrons sitting with them nodded. "Besides, I think it is quite the time you start learning about wifely duties. Being eighteen makes you of marriageable age now. Don't you agree, ladies?" The three older women chuckled at what they presumed was Hannah's nervousness.

"You speak as though I know nothing of men," Hannah protested, "when I have taken care of my father for the past six years."

"Hmmmph," Ruth sounded in response. "I dare say your father has not prepared you for being an obedient wife. Take heed, a husband is not likely to allow you the independence he has encouraged."

Hannah knew going to the church social today was going to be tasking. Nonetheless, she didn't expect the three women to be fussing at her so, but the rumor *had* spread throughout the village. Barnabas was getting close to asking her father for her hand in marriage, and the thought of it made her groan inwardly. The women were right, however. It would be a good match for her. He was the magistrate's son, and she was, after all, just a blacksmith's daughter.

Eleanor did her best to be reassuring. "Don't be so uneasy, dear. Barnabas is an excellent match for you, and not so unpleasant to look at."

"Although I presume he has more than making a good match on his mind. You *are* the fairest maiden around." Ruth poked Hannah's ribs, inspiring a new fit of laughter from the women.

"Ladies, *please* stop teasing me," Hannah murmured. "People are starting to take notice."

"Why, Hannah, you're as red as a beet. Perhaps this sun is too strong for your lovely skin." As usual, Eleanor was unaware of the undercurrent of the teasing.

"You know, ladies," Prudence chimed in, "*I* heard that Barnabas is insisting his father approve the marriage. It's being said that he doesn't even care that our young Hannah has such a modest dowry."

The three of them continued as if they didn't notice Hannah shrinking from embarrassment.

Hannah covered her face with her hands and thought about Barnabas. He was nice enough, she supposed. And, as Eleanor pointed out, he was fair to look upon. They'd known each other since they were children and she had always been aware that he cared deeply about her. But she had never been able to return those feelings. Deep down inside she knew he was *not* the man she wanted to spend the rest of her days and nights with.

She knew he was not that man, because she had seen the one who was.

As happened too often, her thoughts drifted off to another place and time that she could only visit in her dreams. When she was a child, the dreams were about silly, fanciful things. Lately, however, she had been having dreams of a man who aroused her senses just by being nearby, a man who understood the passion she constantly had to restrain within her breast. Night after night he came to her as she slept. He would draw her close and breathe words of love against her throat. Every night, he let down her chestnut brown hair and ran his fingers through it in the same way. In her mind, she replayed the moment when he tilted her head back and brushed his lips against hers.

Hannah felt the blood rush to her cheeks and quickly glanced at the other women. For a few seconds she had completely forgotten where she was, but she clearly had not missed anything. They were still intent on teasing her and were gleefully taking credit for her flushed complexion.

She could not even begin to imagine what they would think if they knew what sort of thoughts danced through her head.

Sinful! Wicked! Wanton!

They would never have such thoughts themselves. Or at least they would never admit to them. Perhaps there *was* something terribly wrong with her, but her dreams did not feel evil. On the contrary, they felt…*right*. And they almost always came to pass in one form or another.

Suddenly, she recalled the dream she'd had last night. The youngest Tompkins boy had been lying on the ground beneath a tree, crying mightily. She looked around until she caught sight of the child and, lo and behold, he had wandered from his family's table unnoticed and was headed for the tallest tree.

"Ladies, I need to quench a sudden thirst. Please excuse me for a moment while I get some lemonade. Would any of you care for some?" When the others declined and continued their chatter, she quickly took her leave. As she walked away she could faintly hear them begin to gossip about one of the other maidens in the village.

Catching up to the wandering boy before he started to climb the tree, she was able to prevent the accident and return him to his family. Once she reached the beverage table, she took her time pouring a cup of liquid refreshment and, thankfully, felt herself cooling off, both from the momentary rush of activity and her former embarrassment.

Confident that she could manage to sit through another hour of gossip, she whirled around to head back to her table, ran right into a man's chest and spilled her cup of lemonade down the front of his jacket.

"Oh my goodness! I am so very sorry. I didn't see you standing there. Oh dear, look what I've done. Here, let me help you." Hannah grabbed a linen cloth from the table and began dabbing at his jacket.

He gently held her wrist and said, "It's all right, really. You needn't apologize. Besides, it was my fault. I was standing right behind you and didn't announce myself."

Hannah looked up and was stunned into silence by the man smiling down at her. He was, without a doubt, the most handsome man she had ever seen. His dark hair and smoky blue eyes held her captive.

And then it hit her. *It's him, the man from my dreams.* Instantly the scene of his mouth descending on hers came back to mind and liquid heat coursed through her veins yet again. Her face flushed and she realized she was staring at him...with her mouth open!

Don't be a fool, Hannah. Say something and stop staring.

"You don't live here," she said more harshly than she'd meant to. *Perfect. Not only have I ruined his jacket and gawked at him, I just snapped at him as well. Oh, I really am a fool!* "I'm sorry that came out a little...I mean...um..." Hannah shook her head in a futile attempt to clear it. "May I be of service in some way?"

He hesitated a moment, as though to be sure she was finished speaking. "Well, actually, I hope you can. I've just arrived and—"

"Good afternoon, Hannah," Barnabas interrupted as he came up behind her. "I think this day is almost as fair as you are." He took her hand and covered it with his own. Facing the stranger, he continued, "How may I assist you, sir?"

The stranger's smile faded. "I'm looking for Reverend Parris. Could you point him out to me?"

"Of course. He's standing over there, talking to those men." Barnabas matter-of-factly waved a hand in their direction. "Hannah, may I escort you back to your table?" Without waiting for a reply, he took her elbow and attempted to lead her away.

"Oh, um…yes, thank you. It was a pleasure meeting you, Mister…"

"Browning. Joseph Browning."

Barnabas tugged a bit harder, which only made her determined to linger. "Yes, as I said, it was a pleasure, Mister Browning. Enjoy your visit to our village." Hannah gave him a sweet smile, aware that it would annoy Barnabas. He should know better than to try to bully her.

"Hannah, you mustn't be so kind to everyone you meet," Barnabas said, continuing to lead her as though she were incapable of finding her own way. "He is not from around here, therefore you do not know what sort of person he is. Sometimes you are simply too trusting of people." He continued to jabber in her ear until they got to her table. Releasing her elbow, he tipped his hat to the women whose conversation had come to an abrupt halt when they saw him approaching. "Good afternoon, ladies. I do hope you are enjoying this delightful weather."

"How could we not?" Ruth leaned forward and, in a hushed voice, asked, "Pray tell us, who is the stranger you were speaking with?"

"He said his name is Browning and he was looking for Reverend Parris, but his eyes seemed a bit…*sly*. Have no fear, I intend to find out his purpose. If you ladies will excuse me…"

"Of course," Ruth replied.

Hannah watched Barnabas head off in the direction he had sent the stranger and relinquished herself to the women once again.

"What did he say to you?" Ruth asked before anyone else could pose a question.

"Did his eyes look sly to you also?" Prudence quickly added.

Eleanor's thoughts were still on an earlier topic. "Did Barnabas say anything about speaking to your father?"

Hannah turned to Eleanor first. "You know it would not be proper for him to discuss such a matter with me, or my father, before he has his own father's approval. And as to Mr. Browning, the only conversation we had pertained to my clumsiness. I spilled lemonade on the poor man and he was assuring me that he was not upset. I have no doubt that Barnabas will let you know more about him shortly."

Having to settle for that, Ruth changed topics. "As I was about to say when you and Barnabas arrived, they arrested Mary Easty two days ago."

"Mary Easty? Whatever for?" Hannah was genuinely surprised.

"What do you think? The same thing everyone else has been arrested for in the past month." Ruth looked from side to side to ensure no one else was listening then whispered, "*Witchcraft.*"

"*No!*" all the women voiced at once.

"Yes. But even worse, yesterday the Salem Magistrates found her guilty."

"This Witch Hunt, as they call it, is becoming a bit worrisome," Eleanor noted with a frown.

"I agree," added Prudence quietly. "Hopefully the fervor will die down before they begin trials for the accused and no serious harm will come of it."

"Let's pray that you are correct," Hannah said, and, for the first time all day, their table fell silent.

The rest of the day went by in a blur. No matter how hard she tried, Hannah could not get Joseph Browning's face out of her head. Before she fell asleep that night she could not help but recall how solid his chest had felt and the way her heart had raced when he held her wrist. Like nothing she had ever felt before...except in her dreams.

When sleep finally came it did not release her from the torment her thoughts had caused. As before, she dreamed of the man coming to her, only this time the dream seemed more real. As his lips brushed over hers, he deepened the kiss and held her closer. Rather than fade off at this point, as the dream usually did, his fingers trailed down her throat and brushed over her breast.

Hannah woke up with a start. *Well,* she thought with a giggle. *That was new.*

The next morning, Hannah could not wait to find out more about the stranger she had run into and knew just the person to get the information from. It took some patience, but when Hannah finally spied Ruth walking down the road, she quickly grabbed the broom kept by the front door and stepped outside. She casually began to sweep the dead leaves off the path leading to her house and waited for Ruth to spot her. Hannah knew that if there was any gossip going around she would be anxious to share it with anyone she saw…and Hannah intended to be in her line of sight.

"Good morning, Hannah," Ruth said as she approached.

"Oh, good morning Ruth. I didn't see you there. How are you today?"

Ruth took a quick look around the area to be certain no one else could hear then led Hannah to the porch. "I found out what that man is doing here."

"Oh?"

"His name is Joseph Browning and he came here from Boston. You may recall that our dear Reverend Parris was going to write letters to several neighboring towns asking if anyone knew of a carpenter who could relocate to our village."

Hannah didn't think there was anyone who spoke as fast as Ruth. "We have been in need of a carpenter, that is for certain."

"Yes, but I learned much more than that. He is a Puritan but has been known to take his faith less seriously than he should. At least he's not one of those Quakers! It is said that he has *traveled* to towns far beyond our colony's borders for reasons unbeknownst to anyone but himself. All quite curious. Your Barnabas may have been correct in thinking he seemed sly."

"That seems—"

"However, because we are in sore need of a carpenter *and* he came with a letter of introduction from his town selectman, the magistrate has decided to allow him to remain."

Barely stopping to take a breath, she continued, "Now, on a personal side, he is a widower. His wife died two years ago giving birth to their stillborn baby, which is said to be one of the reasons why his faith waned. His reverend believed that a move to a new community would benefit him greatly. Sad, isn't it? Ooh, there's Bridget Bishop. I'll see you later, Hannah." Ruth hurried off across the road, waving a handkerchief and calling, "Good morning, Bridget!"

Hannah could hear the town gossip's voice fade to a hush when she reached Bridget and had no doubt that the entire village would soon know about Mr. Browning's curious past. With so much to ponder, Hannah forgot about sweeping and went back inside the house.

Hannah was in the kitchen making the noontime meal when her father walked in with a surprise. "Hannah, dear, please set the table for one more."

As Joseph Browning entered the kitchen behind him, Hannah dropped the ladle into the stew she had been stirring over the fire. She was able to avoid meeting his eyes for several seconds while she recovered the slippery implement. Fortunately, her father did not seem to notice her discomposure.

"This is Joseph Browning, of Boston. He's a carpenter."

She smiled and busied her shaky hands by wiping them on her apron. "Yes, we met at the social yesterday. Welcome again, Mister Browning."

His smile made her feel dizzy and she quickly moved to set the extra place at their table. "Please have a seat."

As she ladled some stew into each of their bowls, her father continued in such a casual tone that she should have suspected something out of the ordinary, but it was all she could do to keep her wits about her.

"The village has made Mister Browning an offer and he has accepted."

"That's good to hear. We all have quite a few repairs that need tending." She found she could say entire sentences without dropping anything as long as she didn't look directly at their guest.

"Yes, that has been a problem. And, as you know, I have also been falling behind in the shop. It was agreed this morning that the family for whom Mister Browning is working will provide his meals for that day."

That sounded like a fine arrangement to her. She drew three cups of water from the bucket and carried two of them to the table.

"And since he will be helping me with my work, he will be staying in the loft above the shop."

She was almost back to the table with her own cup when her father made that announcement. Instantly, the toe of her shoe caught on a loose floorboard and the entire contents of the cup flew through the air — right onto Joseph.

Joseph cleared his throat and calmly brushed away what liquid he could. "Miss Falkner, I am beginning to think that you find some objection to my apparel."

There was no help for it. He was smiling to let her know, once again, that he was not the least bit upset by her clumsiness. Her father looked at her as though she might be having a fit of some sort. And she…well, she was too mortified to speak, so she just sat down and pretended that it was a perfectly normal way to serve a guest a drink in their home.

Bless her father, he had no idea what was wrong but he wanted to fix it. "Hannah, why don't you bring one of my shirts for Mister Browning to change into?"

"Not necessary," Joseph quickly said. "'Tis only water and I'm barely damp. Besides, my own things are in the loft."

His things are in the loft, barely a dozen meters away. His personal belongings, his private things…his undergarments. Are his things different from Father's? Will I be doing his laundry as well as preparing his meals? Dear God in heaven, how am I supposed to manage such a task when I cannot even serve him a cup of water?

"Another benefit to our providing Mister Browning with lodgings is that he will begin by patching the hole in the roof over your bed. Why don't you make a list of things we need to have done. I'm certain that is what the other women will be doing today." He took a bite of his food and continued, "I must tell you, Mister Browning, despite your unfortunate experience with my Hannah, she is the one who has always kept this house from falling down around my ears. Losing her mother would have been unbearable if not for her."

"I understand," Joseph said seriously. "After I lost my wife, it was difficult for me to get on for quite a while."

Hannah wanted to say something appropriate, but her mind was filled with molasses.

"You're a very good cook, Hannah," Joseph said. "I hope my work will please you enough to earn quite a few of your meals."

Hannah froze. He wanted to please her. She was not entirely certain what that meant, but she could think of nothing she wanted more at that moment.

Clear those thoughts, silly girl. Do you want him to think you're the village idiot?

She took a slow breath. "Thank you. We are very fortunate to have you first, I mean, have you here, working for us first, before any of the other villagers..." She clamped her mouth shut before any more nonsense escaped.

After one last bite of stew, her father rose and said, "And knowing that everyone will be anxious for their turn, we'd best get started. We'll visit more when we return for supper." He gave Hannah a quick peck on her forehead and left the kitchen.

Joseph hesitated for a moment. "I'm sorry, Hannah."

She blinked at him. "I beg your pardon?"

"I have not spent much time around maidens these last few years. I did not realize my presence here would cause you distress. Would you prefer that I make other arrangements?"

"No!" she blurted out much too quickly. "I mean, certainly not. It is clearly to our advantage to have you stay with us and I can see that my father is truly looking forward to having your help in his shop. I honestly do not know what has gotten into me. I am not usually so clumsy."

His sincere expression altered into a charming grin. "Good. Then perhaps it is just my being near you that makes you unsteady. I cannot deny a certain pleasure in knowing that."

Even more confused than she was before, she watched him turn and walk out while she stood there, totally speechless…and totally captivated.

Every day at mid-afternoon, she brought a pitcher of cool lemonade next door for her father. There were days in the winter when she would sit by the fiery forge for hours and watch him work, but as the days grew warmer, she found the heat intolerable. As she entered the shop, the blast of heat seemed worse than usual, though her discomfort might have been caused by something else entirely.

She had thought Joseph was up on the roof, and it was safe for her to go into the shop. However, he was there, helping her father. Perspiration had his white shirt clinging to his back, revealing the sinuous movement of his muscles as he swung the heavy hammer down onto a horseshoe on the anvil. She had seen her father do the exact same thing a thousand times, but never had she been so fascinated by the simple act.

Suddenly she realized that her father was looking at her, but this time he did not seem so confused by her peculiar behavior. A moment later, Joseph turned around to see what her father was looking at.

She didn't understand how a man could be drenched in sweat and still seem so interesting. His lips turned up in a smile, revealing his perfect white teeth. If only one or two of them were missing, then perhaps she wouldn't be so bewitched.

Oh dear, I'm staring at his mouth...that mouth that has touched mine in... Stop! I'm doing it again! Don't just stand here gaping. Do something. No, say something. No, do something. The lemonade! Yes, that's it. I brought lemonade. Just give them the lemonade.

Without a word, she set down the pitcher and scurried back into the house.

As she finished her afternoon chores and prepared supper, Hannah gave herself a stern talking-to and was certain she could keep her wits about her the next time she saw Joseph. That certainty lasted right up to the moment he entered the kitchen, all washed up and smelling like soap.

"That smells very good," he said as he walked over to where she was stirring the leftover stew. He stopped just short of making physical contact with her then inhaled deeply.

She stopped stirring, afraid that the slightest movement on her part could result in disaster.

He slowly eased away from her then sat down at the table. "We had a good day today. I believe your father was pleased."

"Pleased?" her father echoed as he came to the table. "I can hardly believe how much we got done together. Hannah, this man had me working like I was his age again!"

She let out the breath she'd been holding. "That is very good to hear. Where will you be working tomorrow, Mister Browning?"

"I am promised to the magistrate in the morning, but I will be available in the afternoon. Shall I work on your roof or is there something else you would prefer I do to earn my supper?"

The look in his eyes suggested he had a fair idea of what she would prefer, and that made her even more nervous.

* * * * *

Over the next month, Joseph spent part of his time working on other villagers' houses and shops. The rest of his time was given to the Falkners, either doing carpentry work or helping in the blacksmith shop. Whenever he had a meal at their table, he was polite and grateful, but more surprising to Hannah was that he was entertaining. Joseph had the gift of finding humor in the most ordinary events.

Once he learned that Hannah and her father were both interested in hearing about his travels, he had an endless supply of stories to tell them. After his wife's death, he had wandered from place to place for a while, all the way south to Jamestown in the colony of Virginia, before returning to Boston.

As the weeks passed, Hannah slowly became less agitated by Joseph's presence. She still felt different around him, but it was not in any way bad. She had even managed to stop dropping or spilling things when he was near. Best of all, she regained her ability to speak as though there were a brain in her head.

One evening, as the three of them were finishing dinner, Joseph was regaling them with a story that had her giggling like a young girl.

"And there I was, standing between the prize pig and its freedom. I thought it would be a simple matter of picking it up and walking off with it, but it ran straight toward me. I tried to block its escape but it got under my feet and the next thing I knew, I was lying in mud and the pig was standing on my chest as though *it* had captured *me* instead. Meanwhile, there was my friend standing a safe distance off, perfectly unsullied and having a mighty laugh, when he was the one who had the idea to capture the squealing beast in the first place!"

Hannah held her sides as she laughed. "I think that may be the funniest story yet. I wish I could have been there to have witnessed it."

"I wish you could have as well."

Hannah stopped laughing as she noticed the change in his gaze. He was looking at her mouth the way he did in her dreams and she felt her insides soften.

A knock at the door saved her from making a fool of herself in front of her father.

"Enter," her father said, still chuckling.

"I heard such laughter as I was—" Barnabas stopped speaking—and smiling—the instant he noticed Joseph.

Ignoring his childish pout, Hannah quickly rose to her duty as mistress. "Will you have some supper? Or tea, perhaps?"

Barnabas pulled his gaze away from Joseph and forced a smile for Hannah. "No thank you." He stiffly turned to her father. "Goodman Falkner, I was actually coming to ask if you would join us for a meeting at the church this evening. There is something of importance that is being discussed and I thought to accompany you myself. But I seem to have interrupted something of importance here…"

"Not at all," the elder insisted as he rose from the table. "We are just finished. Give me a moment to fetch my jacket."

Hannah could almost hear Barnabas' thoughts. He was disturbed to find Joseph at their table and even more so to be leaving her alone with the sly one, without the watchful eye of her father. But since Joseph was still considered a stranger by most, he would not be welcome at a village meeting.

For a few heartbeats after the two men left, neither Hannah nor Joseph uttered a word. They both knew it was not proper to be alone in this manner, but her father had not instructed him to leave.

"Perhaps I should go," Joseph offered hesitantly.

"Perhaps," she agreed, just as carefully. "But I would not mind if you stayed and told me another story while I clean up." She picked up their plates and took them to the bucket of soapy water.

He stood up and followed her, carrying their cups. "I have noted that my presence no longer causes you to spill things."

She smiled at him. "I have no idea why that kept happening."

"You don't?" He set the cups down then took both her hands in his. With the slightest pressure of his thumbs he drew her gaze up to meet his.

She felt the warmth of his hands blending with her own and her heart picked up its pace. Her lips parted as though she had something to say, but no words came to mind.

Joseph brought her hands up between them and lightly touched his lips to her knuckles. "I have something other than a story that I would like to tell you."

A swallow and a blink was the only response she could manage.

Continuing to hold her hands against his chest, he said, "I cared for my wife. Our families were neighbors and considered us an appropriate match. She was a kind woman but always seemed sad. She spent more time praying to God than talking to me. I grieved when she died, both for her loss and that of our stillborn babe. But part of my pain was because I was never able to bring a smile to her face, no matter how hard I tried.

"Hannah, when you laugh, it's like a ray of sunshine has come into the room. It's why I keep telling so many stories. Your laughter has made me feel alive again. You are the most beautiful woman I have ever encountered. From the first moment I saw you, I felt as though something new was born inside of me, and it's been growing stronger each day." He released one of her hands so that he could stroke her cheek with his fingertips. "As soft as I imagined."

"You truly should not…" His fingers trailed down the side of her throat and she could not remember what she was about to say.

"No, I should not. But I can no longer obey the rules of propriety when I am given such an opportunity as this." He slid his hand back up her arm and placed a finger under her chin, tilting her head back just a bit more. He gazed deeply into her eyes then murmured, "And I do not see a protest here."

Her eyelids lowered and a sigh of submission escaped on a soft breath. She had dreamed of this moment so often that she wondered if it was real or if she was once again lost in one of her musings.

Thankfully, he did not make her wait long to find out. As in her dream, his lips brushed softly back and forth over hers, then ever so tenderly, his mouth pressed more firmly. It was that delicious pressure that assured her that she was not dreaming and a tiny moan of pleasure rose in her throat as she responded in kind.

When he eased away she tried to follow, but his fingertip touched her lips to stay her. She opened her eyes and saw him smiling down at her. He looked as happy as she felt.

"I know I said I wanted to ignore propriety, but I would not have you regretting our first kiss in the morning. I give you fair warning though, my sweet, you could distract a man out of his best intentions, so I would ask you to help me remember your innocence in the future. I believe I have begun to earn your father's respect and I will do my best to be patient until sufficient time has passed for him to be comfortable with the idea of my formally courting you. But now, as much as it pains me to leave while you have that look in your eyes, I must, for both our sakes." He gave her one quick peck on her nose and walked out of her house.

Hannah stood unmoving for a very long time after he'd gone. She knew what they had just done was considered to be wrong, forbidden, lustful and probably a dozen more words that could banish her to hell. But she could not find a dram of guilt in her heart. All she could think about was, how long would she have to wait to do it again?

Chapter Seven

At the church social the next day, Hannah sat down at her usual table with Ruth, Eleanor and Prudence. The prattling about other people's affairs had already begun. She looked around the crowd and noticed Barnabas talking to her father and wondered what they might be discussing. Her father had come home late last night and did not mention anything about the meeting he'd attended. She thought he seemed disturbed then, and now he looked decidedly uncomfortable. Then again, Barnabas always did have the ability to drone on and on about a subject long after his audience had lost interest.

Continuing to discreetly scan the area, her gaze lit on Joseph. He was seated at a table with several men, all talking and laughing. She inwardly smiled as she watched him following the conversation. As though she had called his name aloud, he turned his head toward her and grinned.

"Then she told him that if he had such a problem with her mother visiting, he could just sleep with the horse!" Ruth slapped her palm on the table as all three women shook with laughter.

The loud noise jerked Hannah's thoughts back to them. To cover her inattention, she let out a chuckle and repeated, "With the horse?"

"In the stable!" Prudence confirmed. "And the horse woke him up in the morning by licking his face!" That picture had them all laughing again.

Eleanor furrowed her brow. "I'm not sure we should be gossiping about such private matters."

"Oh Eleanor," Ruth replied firmly. "How many times have I told you it's not *gossiping*. It's more like…passing along information that others may need to hear. There are good lessons to be learned from the experiences of others."

"Speaking of others," Prudence said, changing the subject. "The four of us should pay a visit to Goody Easty before she is sent to the prison in Boston. I think it is our duty to let her know there are some of us who still believe she is a good woman. I don't want her to feel alone and I'm sure she would appreciate some good food as well."

"I don't understand," Hannah said, obviously confused. "Wasn't Goody Easty released from the jail last week?"

Ruth looked at her, surprised. "Hannah, where have you been? She *was* released, but when Mercy Lewis fell ill again, Mary Easty was accused of causing the illness."

Hannah couldn't believe what she was hearing. How could she not have known about this? Had she really been so immersed in her fascination with Joseph that she missed something this important?

A few minutes later the four women headed down the road with a basket for the prisoner.

When they arrived at the small barn that had been recently converted by Joseph to serve as a temporary jail, Ruth stepped forward and spoke to the guard in her most authoritative voice. "We have come to visit Goody Easty. Would you be kind enough to take us to her?"

The guard pondered a moment before relenting. "I suppose there be no harm in that. Be careful not to look directly in her eyes, lest you be afflicted by her as well. She's the third door on the left. But if anyone asks, I was not the one who let you in."

"Of course not," Ruth answered and led the women inside.

They stopped in front of the large wooden door and Ruth peered through the small opening.

"Can you see her?" whispered Eleanor.

"Is someone out there?" Mary asked fearfully from within the cell.

"Yes, dear," answered Ruth. "It's Sunday. And since you could not attend church, we've come to pray with you here."

Mary's face appeared in the opening and Hannah said, "We were worried about you and wanted to make sure you were well."

"We brought you food!" Eleanor stated, proud of the fact that they had accomplished such a secret feat.

"We assumed you would not be fed properly and wanted to bring you some sustenance," Prudence added as she passed the food through the opening.

"Oh, thank you so much, ladies," Mary said, taking the gifts as though they were valuable treasures. "You are truly friends. But I fear that this shadow they have placed on me may cast doubt over you. You did not need to do this, but I am very grateful for your visit."

Ruth wasted no time before voicing her curiosity. "We heard that you are being blamed for Mercy's illness. What happened?"

"Sadly," Mary answered, "you know about as much as I do right now. I thought I had been cleared of all the false charges against me. They told me I was free to return home, that they no longer believed me to be a witch. Then, two days later, they came pounding on my door accusing me all over again."

"This is too terrible to be true," Eleanor said.

"I didn't even have the chance to visit my sister," Mary added. "She was arrested and sent to a prison in Boston before they came after me the first time. I so wanted to know she was all right."

"Don't worry yourself over Rebecca," Hannah responded. "I am sure she will be fine. You both will. These actions are wrong and the good people will see that."

"I simply do not understand why I have been accused," Mary said with a catch in her throat. "I have never afflicted any person before. I don't believe I have ever done a single thing to cause harm to another person, not even as an accident. I pray to

God that if there are witches amongst us, let them be found, but they need to release those of us who are completely innocent."

The guard came up behind the four women and interrupted their visit. "Ladies, it's time you be moving on now."

"A brief moment more, kind sir. We were about to say a prayer for Goody Easty's soul." He took a few steps back and bowed his head as the four women said a prayer together.

As soon as "amen" was spoken, the guard insisted they leave. Ruth had no choice this time but to reluctantly obey. The women said their goodbyes to Mary and headed quietly back to their homes.

* * * * *

"How did your visit go today?" Hannah's father asked while they were having their nightly cup of tea.

She shook her head. "Not well. I truly do not understand what is happening in our village. Mary Easty is no more a witch than am I."

"That was debated at last night's meeting, but Reverend Parris is well respected and he is convinced that witchcraft is being practiced right beneath our noses. The Village Committee is supporting the continuation of the hunt."

"Then I will pray very hard that God grant them greater wisdom."

"On another matter," her father said pointedly, "did you see Barnabas talking to me today?"

"Yes, and you looked like you were thoroughly enjoying your conversation."

He grimaced. "Your sense of humor is developing in a very peculiar way of late. As a matter of fact, Barnabas was speaking to me about a noticeable difference in your behavior."

"Oh?" She tried to sound indifferent, but her stomach was churning.

"He informed me that he has noticed you are no longer as attentive to him as you once were. He has determined that it must be because you have grown tired of being a maiden."

Hannah guessed what was coming and prayed that she was mistaken.

"Hannah, he formally requested that the two of you be publicly betrothed."

She closed her eyes and tried to think of how she could tell her father of her feelings for Joseph, without his thinking poorly of her. "What about his father's disapproval of me as a match?"

"It seems that even his own father can only stand so much of his constant badgering. Oh my, you are suddenly looking very pale. You really should have a little faith in your father, dear."

Taking another sip of tea, he continued, "I put him off. The two of you may have known each other for a long time, but I can see the way you look at him, and it is not with love. I understand that notions of love are not to be considered when arranging a marriage, but I want you to have the chance to experience the deep affection your mother and I shared. I know you wouldn't be happy with him and that is all that matters to me."

Her eyes widened and she felt the color return to her face. "What did you tell him?"

"That ever since your mother died, you have taken on the responsibility of mistress of my house and that I could not manage without you just yet. He was disappointed, but hopefully his attention will soon turn to another maiden. Perhaps the one his father had already selected."

"Oh Father, thank you." Hannah visibly relaxed and finally began to enjoy her tea. She and Joseph would still have time to prepare him for their news.

Smiling, he continued, "Don't thank me. I was serious. I would be completely lost and this house would go to pieces without you."

"I know you would manage fine without me, but I will surely be with you for a while yet."

"Don't be daft, girl. Do you think that I am unaware of what is going on beneath my own roof?"

The kiss she and Joseph shared instantly came to mind and her cheeks flamed. "What do you mean?"

"What do I mean? My dear child, you give yourself away every time you see him."

He isn't aware of the kiss. She relaxed a little. "I confess that I have a sudden weakness when Mister Browning is near."

Setting his tea down, her father rose from his chair and slowly paced across the room. "Joseph seems to be a good man…kind, honorable and a hard worker. Though he is not of our village, he is still of our faith. But most importantly, I can see he cares for you. I suspect that he's been giving thought to courting you. And in due time I will give him my approval, if you'll have him."

"But—"

"Let me finish. I know he makes you nervous, but it is perfectly normal for a maiden to have such a reaction. All I am trying to say is open your eyes and see what is right in front of you. Now, it's been a long day and I'm going to bed. Promise to think about what I've said." He leaned down and gave her a kiss on the forehead.

"I promise." Hannah's happiness knew no bounds as she watched her father walk away.

* * * * *

Joseph was kept so busy over the next several days that Hannah had not been able to tell him of the conversation with her father. Finally on the second day of June, because he came in to fetch the afternoon lemonade before she could bring it to the shop, they were granted a brief spell of time together.

The moment she saw him walk into the kitchen alone, her heart skipped a beat. Not wanting to waste a single second, he marched straight over to her, pulled her into his arms, kissed her soundly then released her just as quickly.

"I'm sorry to be so hasty, but I have thought of little else but kissing you these last few days and your father will expect me to return in a moment."

She smiled. "I also have had difficulty forgetting...but I have something very important to tell you. My father—" She was interrupted by loud voices outside. The commotion increased until they could not resist investigating the disturbance.

As they stepped out the front door, they saw that a crowd had gathered in front of Bridget Bishop's house and she was being pulled along by several members of the Village Committee.

Before they had a chance to ask anyone what was going on, Ruth came rushing toward them. "You won't believe it. You just won't believe it. *I* can't believe it."

"Believe what, Ruth? What's going on?" Hannah asked.

Taking a moment to catch her breath, Ruth continued, "They just arrested Bridget for witchcraft!"

"*What?* That can't be, there must be some mistake!"

"Who is her accuser?" Joseph asked.

"Susannah Sheldon," Ruth answered. "But even worse, Bridget is not the only one she has accused today. Susannah pointed her finger at Mary English and Giles Corey as well. She claims their spectres appeared before her during the night and told her of their evil. They are arresting Bridget first because it was said that her being widowed so many times is proof enough of guilt. I overheard them saying they were taking her directly to the meetinghouse in Salem to start her trial immediately."

"Trial?" questioned Joseph. "They have yet to put any of the accused on trial."

"Yes, I know. But that was because they had no court to try them. Well, as of six days ago, that situation was corrected. Governor Phips created the Court of Oyer and Terminer to deal with all these horrible accusations. Bridget is to be the first to appear before them. It will be open to the public and I intend to be there." She turned from them and headed toward someone else who appeared to be uninformed.

As the crowd moved farther down the road, Joseph led Hannah back inside the house.

"This is wrong. Very, very wrong," Hannah said as she paced the floor. "Bridget is a good woman. She doesn't deserve to have this happen to her."

"I know."

"I should have done something to stop it, or better yet I should have warned her so she could leave the area. They would not have been able to arrest her then."

"Hannah, what are you talking about? How could you have given her a warning? You didn't even know this was happening."

Hannah turned and walked quickly toward him. "Joseph, I need to know that if I tell you something you will never tell another soul as long as you live."

"Of course, Hannah. What's going on?"

"You see, I have these dreams."

"Everyone has dreams."

"Not like mine. I don't really know how to explain it, but in my dreams I see things. Things that haven't happened yet." The puzzled look on his face told her she needed to explain further. "For example, before you came to our village, I dreamed of you, every night for several weeks. I would see your face, clear as it is right now. Then one day, I turned around and there you were, standing right in front of me."

"You dreamt of me?"

She nodded. "But there's more."

"I'm listening."

"Because of these dreams, I can usually stop bad things from happening to others. For instance, I've given warnings to Barnabas several times and once I was even able to warn him in time to save his mare's life."

"Does he know about your dreams?"

"No, he would never understand. I find ways of explaining my, uh...*suggestions* other than the truth. I believe God forgives me for such small fibs as long as the outcome is for someone else's benefit. My father is the only one who knows. He said my mother had strange dreams as well."

"And yet you trust me."

"Yes, I do." She crossed the room and looked out the window toward Bridget's house. "I saw the crowd dragging her away. I heard them calling her a witch. But I thought it was just my dream getting mixed up with visiting Mary Easty. I should have done something for Bridget but I couldn't imagine how that dream could possibly come true."

Joseph walked up behind Hannah, wrapped his arms around her and held her in a protective embrace. "This is not your fault. If you really thought they were going to arrest her, I know you would have done something to help. But be honest with yourself. If you had told her this would happen, would she have believed you and left the village? Or might she have accused *you* of being a witch instead? With everything that's been happening in this colony, it would not be safe for you to reveal that you have dreams of things to come."

He turned her in his arms and wiped a tear from her cheek. "I have acquaintances in Boston and Salem. I will write to them and see what is being done for the others. Perhaps there is someone helping these poor women."

Those words helped her to forgive herself. She put her arms around his waist and placed her head on his chest. "Thank you."

"Do you feel a little better?"

"A little."

He tipped her head back and pressed a light but lingering kiss on her mouth. After another moment he asked, "How about now?"

"Much better," Hannah whispered as she leaned back to look at him.

"Good, because I've made it my mission in life to make you happy."

"Truly?" she asked innocently.

He kissed her again, this time a bit more seriously. "Truly. But you will have to do a few things to make me happy as well."

She felt the heat rising in her body. "Pray, kind sir, what sort of things might I do to please you?"

His grin was wicked and irresistible at the same time. "To begin with, I have been wondering what you would look like with your hair hanging loose." With strained control, Joseph slowly removed her cap and unbound her hair. As he watched it tumble down her back he said, "And I thought you could not be more beautiful." Pressing her close once more, he captured her mouth in another heated kiss.

Hannah felt as though she was being set on fire. It was her dream all over again. She sighed and Joseph pulled her body more tightly against his. "I know you are too innocent to understand what you do to me, but you needn't be afraid."

She looked directly in his eyes and framed his face with her hands. "I am only afraid that I will perish if you do not kiss me as you have in my dreams."

When he saw that the fever in her eyes matched his own, his mouth closed on hers in earnest. She had never imagined that a kiss could involve one's entire body but there was not a piece of her that did not feel like it was melting into him.

He undid several buttons on her bodice so that he could caress her throat with his lips, and as he did so, his hand eased farther down over her breast. Assured that her gasp was more pleasure than surprise, he gently kneaded the flesh that he hoped to soon uncover.

As much as she liked that, she was not ready for him to stop kissing her. Threading her fingers into his hair, she drew his face back to hers. As their kiss deepened, his tongue slid into her mouth, increasing her pleasure so much that she gave it a light suck.

His reaction was a low groan as he grabbed her bottom and lifted her up against him. Only when Hannah tried to wrap her legs around him did he realize how far they had gone.

"Hannah, my love, you're undoing me." He eased her back to her feet and held her at arm's length as he struggled to catch his breath.

She blinked at him several times before her brain reconnected with her body. Then it all hit her at once. They were standing in front of the window. Anyone could have seen them! She quickly glanced in both directions but saw no one nearby. "My father! He must be wondering what happened to you. He could have come in at any moment. What would I have done? What could I have said? I mean, he approves of us, he told me as much, but still—"

"He approves?" Joseph asked with surprise. "You're certain? I could ask his permission and he wouldn't laugh in my face?"

Hannah was busy re-buttoning her bodice and tucking her hair back up under her cap, but it pleased her that he looked happy about the news, even if she hadn't delivered it quite as well as she had planned.

He leaned down and brushed his lips against hers. "I must be going, but I will speak to your father after church on Sunday, as would be proper." Turning to leave, he gave her one last meaningful grin and said, "Oh and Hannah...you're going to love being my wife."

* * * * *

Jezebel! That's who she is—the Devil's Temptress, with a pretty face to seduce a virtuous man! How dare she behave in such a wanton manner! I defied my own father to give her the honor of being my wife, but she'd rather play the whore for that...that stranger! I'll show her! I'll soon have her begging me for forgiveness!

The image of what Barnabas had witnessed through Hannah's front window would not fade from his mind. He had only thought to check on her welfare following her neighbor's arrest, but from what he saw, her welfare was being thoroughly attended to—by another man. His seething rage began to calm only as he came up with a plan to deal with Hannah's treachery.

* * * * *

That night, Hannah's dreams were so upsetting she awoke more tired than when she had lain down. Gray clouds hid most of the details. The only thing she saw clearly was Joseph, locked behind the jail door where Mary had been held. He was reaching his arm through, as if trying to squeeze out. She heard him scream her name and saw tears running down his face.

Several days later, Hannah was outside hanging laundry when she noticed a number of the Committee members walking down the road with great determination. *What could they possibly be up to now?* Her curiosity turned to a cold chill when they marched right up to her and stopped.

"We have a warrant for your arrest," her longtime neighbor informed her. "Please come with us."

"What? What are you talking about? You must be mistaken." When Hannah realized the man was completely serious, she changed her tone to indignation. "On what charges?"

"On the charges of witchcraft."

"*Witchcraft?* That is absolutely absurd. Who is my accuser?"

"We are not at liberty to say at this time. You must come with us now."

"Wait. Please—"

"What is the meaning of this!" Hannah's father shouted as he rushed out of his shop. He was instantly blocked by several villagers.

"Stand back, Goodman Falkner. Your daughter has been accused of witchcraft and must be locked up for all of our protection."

The men encircled Hannah and prodded her along to the makeshift jail. She could see her neighbors peering out their windows and coming outside to see what was happening, exactly as she had done when Bridget Bishop was arrested.

Bridget, a friend and neighbor, a good, kindhearted woman, who was tried by a new court the same day of her arrest and immediately sentenced to hang on Gallows Hill.

Was that to be her fate as well? Arrested, tried and accused in the passing of a single day? Had God suddenly taken his protection away from the good women of Salem Village?

She tried not to think of it, but was it possible that God had not approved of her thoughts about Joseph or her lustful behavior with him, despite the fact that they intended to be wed?

No! she heard as loudly as though someone had shouted in her ear. This is not God's doing. It is the Devil's. And may God forgive those who have been blinded by the powers of Lucifer.

* * * * *

Because Joseph had been working for a family on the outskirts of the village, he did not hear the news for several hours. The moment it reached him, he ran all the way to the blacksmith's shop. Hannah's father was just sitting there, staring at the fire. "Is it true?" he blurted out.

The man nodded. "They took her away and wouldn't let me go with her. They intend to try her regardless of how absurd it is."

"We need to do something. Quickly. Before she is taken to court."

"I agree, but what can we do?"

"What do you mean? The magistrate is your friend. His son Barnabas has been Hannah's friend since they were children. You can talk to him. He knows she isn't capable of anything wicked."

"I just came from his house," her father said quietly. "Barnabas is the accuser."

"What?" Joseph shook his head in disbelief. "How could he say such a—" Joseph stopped short as realization set in. He remembered the expression on Barnabas' face when he saw them having dinner together. But would the man's jealousy actually be so strong to make him do something this terrible?

"Barnabas told his father that Hannah was in league with the Devil, that Satan himself told her of things that would later come to pass. Apparently, Hannah gave Barnabas a warning or two of events before they happened."

"Yes, she mentioned something about saving a mare's life."

Her father raised a brow. "She must trust you very much to have told you about that. It was just one time of many when she warned Barnabas of a problem before it arose. At first, the magistrate refused to accept what his son was saying, so Barnabas stirred up others with his tales. Hannah would never harm a soul. The warnings she gave were only meant to help, and now her good deeds are being used against her."

"There were others whom she gave warnings to besides Barnabas?"

"Unfortunately, yes. And once he roused concern, nearly every person in the village came forward with some report of Hannah knowing the future before it happened. She is not evil, but neither is Bridget Bishop, and they have already set a date next week for her hanging."

"Don't worry, sir. I'll figure something out. I refuse to allow any harm to come to her."

"You care deeply for my daughter, don't you?"

"No, sir. I *love* your daughter deeply. And when this is over, I intend to ask for her hand."

"In that case, you have my permission, on one condition."

"Anything."

"Get her out of their clutches, any way you can, and take her far from here. I would rather never see her face again and know she's safe than to lose her to a hangman's noose."

* * * * *

"Hannah…Hannah wake up. Hannah, please wake up, I don't have a lot of time."

Hannah awoke as soon as she heard Joseph's husky whisper. It took her a moment to realize that he was outside. She quickly rose and moved to the small barred window that gave her a tiny view of the outside world. "I'm so happy to see you. Have you brought news?"

"I must be honest. The news is not good. Barnabas is behind this. It's my opinion that he did not accept your father's refusal for your hand as easily as you thought. Now he is using your past kindness to prove your guilt. Your father and I have come up with a way to help you escape. I will come for you tomorrow night, but you must understand that we will have to disappear until this witch hunt is over."

"We?"

"Yes, Hannah. *We.* I intend on getting you out of here and spending the rest of our days fulfilling the promise I made you."

"Promise?"

"Yes, Hannah. The promise I made that you will love being married to me." Joseph kissed his fingertips and reached through the bars to touch her lips. "I'll see you tomorrow night, my sweet."

"Tomorrow night," Hannah said as she watched him disappear from her view.

* * * * *

Joseph awoke to something tickling his nose then felt the furious pounding in his head. It was dark. He blinked several times before being able to fully understand his circumstances. He was sprawled face-down on a bed of hay, his mouth gagged, his hands tied behind his back and his ankles bound. He suddenly remembered something hard slamming into his head before everything went black.

"I see you are finally starting to wake up," someone whispered.

He wriggled onto his side to see who was speaking and growled ferociously when he recognized Barnabas. A hard kick in the stomach warned Joseph not to make idle threats.

Barnabas' voice remained hushed as he explained. "There are rules, Mister Browning. Rules that you have blatantly ignored. You have come to our village as a stranger and have been welcomed. Yet you have the audacity to steal what is not yours."

Joseph growled again and was dealt another swift kick.

"You will respond only when I give permission. You will not speak or make noise of any kind. If you do so again, Hannah will suffer the punishment instead of you. And you will hear her cries. For, you see, her cell is three away from this one, and I want you to know the feeling of her being so close yet not even knowing that you are here. Just as I have been treated by her for so very long. Then you arrived, and she freely gave to you what she never considered giving to me."

Barnabas turned his back on Joseph and seemed to be talking to himself for a moment. "*Me!* The man who waited for her to mature. The man who was devoted to her every whim his entire life. The man who would have married beneath his station to have her. But she never cared. It was her father's fault of course. He gave her liberties a woman should never know."

The enraged man whirled back around but kept his voice to a whisper as he continued. "I knew the Devil spoke to her, you see, but I never would have told anyone. Then you arrived and I was finally forced to acknowledge the whore she truly is. I was not blaming you, of course. You are made of flesh and bone and must suffer the weaknesses of being vulnerable to a Jezebel such as she. But I cannot allow you to help her escape the punishment God has decreed.

"I knew you would visit her. I suspected that you might be tempted to help her escape. And now that I caught you in the act, you will be officially arrested and tried as well. You gave in to the Devil's wiles and now must accept your fate. She will hang and you will not be able to prevent it."

* * * * *

Every night for the next week, Hannah waited for Joseph to show up, to no avail. She had complete faith that he would come for her if he possibly could, but at the same time, she could not forget the awful dream she'd had about his being imprisoned. The days had gone by with no visitors whatsoever, except the guard with her daily meal and a clean bucket, and he would not even look at her let alone answer her questions. She had no idea why she had not yet been taken to Salem or Boston, as the other men and women had. It gave her a small hope that Barnabas' accusation was being reconsidered.

The other thing which was curious to her was that, from time to time, she heard noises that gave her the impression there was someone else in the jail besides herself. However, when she called out, no one responded.

Her wait for something to happen ended on the evening of June 10. A rising hum of voices outside drew her to the window. Standing on tiptoes, Hannah saw a throng of villagers striding determinedly toward the jail carrying lanterns and torches. She froze in terror when she realized the man at the head of the crowd was carrying rope, and her tiny hope that she would be freed vanished in an instant.

A moment later the guard unlocked her door and spoke to her for the first time since she had been imprisoned. "Come, miss. It is time to pay for your sins."

"Am I being taken to Boston?" Hannah asked despite the evidence outside.

Rather than reply he grasped her arm and pulled her out of the cell. As she was leaving, she distinctly heard a muffled voice coming from a few cells behind her, but the guard yanked her along.

As soon as she stepped outside, the leader of the crowd loudly cried out, "Hannah Falkner, you have been accused of the crime of witchcraft and been found guilty by your peers."

"How could I be found guilty? There has been no trial!"

"The Court of Oyer and Terminer determined Bridget Bishop's guilt and she was this morn hung by the neck until dead."

Oh dear God! They really did it. "What has that to do with the accusations against my person?"

"Your case has been reviewed and it has been decided that you are far more dangerous than Goody Bishop ever was. We cannot risk the possibility that you will use your powers to blind the court to your guilt. We are here to make certain that you shall never have the opportunity to endanger our innocent souls again."

"Hang the witch!" someone shouted, and the mob took up the cry as they dragged Hannah away from the jail.

Barnabas jerked Joseph to his feet and shoved him against the wall of the cell. "I want you to see what you have done to her." He forced his face against the bars of the window.

Joseph protested beneath his gag.

"I suppose it will do no harm now," Barnabas said and yanked down the rag.

"You bastard!" Joseph strained his unused voice. "Stop them! You know she is no witch."

"On the contrary, I believe I was thoroughly bewitched. Anyway, I'm afraid it is out of my hands."

Joseph stared in horror as the rope was being tied to a thick branch of a tree in the field beyond the jail. He was frantic to come up with anything that would stop the scene before him. He turned his head away and tried to reason with Barnabas. "Your father could stop them. She should be made to stand trial like the others." As Joseph realized it was far too late for reason, tears welled up in his eyes and he pleaded, "Let me stand in her place and the Committee can order her father to take her away from your village. He would do that gladly."

Barnabas roughly turned his head forward again and held it there this time. "I said you will watch this. As to *your* hanging...be patient. Your turn will come in due time."

Joseph's mind reeled in panic as he saw them force Hannah to stand upon a crate. When they drew the noose over her head, he could take no more. *"Hannah!"* he cried out, despite knowing that the roar of the mob would drown out his hoarse voice.

But as they tightened the noose around her throat, she turned her head toward his jail cell and he knew that she felt him there, helpless to save her. A moment later, the crate was kicked away and he felt the pain as keenly as if the rope had snapped his own neck instead of hers.

"Noooooo!"

Chapter Eight

"How are you feeling?"

Leilani latched onto Phyllis' voice like a lifeline and slowly found her way back into her body. She noticed a tissue had been placed in her hand and dabbed at the trickle of tears that had flowed from her eyes. "That was more...intense than the first one, that's for sure. I'm emotionally wiped out...as if it just happened."

"Not unusual," Phyllis replied. "Each time you go back, it does get easier *and* more realistic. First-time subjects, even if they don't mean to, tend to keep a tighter hold on their present physical reality, so they maintain a somewhat objective viewpoint. As their trust in the process increases, they loosen up on one life and go more deeply into the other."

"Well, I definitely felt like I was there...especially with him."

"Have you ever watched a movie or read a book that was so well done that you cried when the heroine's heart was broken or thrilled when the hero saved the day?"

"Of course." Leilani sniffed, still trying to shake off the sadness. "Oh, I see. This was even worse because it wasn't sympathy for some fictional character, it was real to me. I was actually, *personally*, remembering the love and the terror."

"Exactly. But keep in mind that you've probably also had lives with very happy endings. It just so happens your question has taken you down two tragic paths."

"No kidding. One thing seems obvious. That's twice that the poor guy had to stand by while I got killed in a pretty awful way. Considering my dreams, it looks like it could be his turn to die...and my turn to — "

"Uh-uh. Don't even *think* those words. History does *not* have to repeat itself. That's why we're doing this—to prevent something terrible from happening again."

"I understand, and I do see how the two sessions have shown the sort of karmic issue involved, but I'm no closer to figuring out who or where the present-day man is!" Leilani realized how annoyed she sounded. "I'm sorry. I'm just terribly frustrated."

Phyllis smiled. "No need to apologize, but you're wrong. You have already stopped him from fading away and you have an extra piece to your mystery. The date might be more of a key than you first realized. Perhaps your next dream will supply a location or his name. And if you still don't get it, I'll make time for you to have a third session over the weekend."

"Third time's the charm?" Leilani felt her mood lighten. "Okay. I'll let you know." She rose to leave then remembered a question. "I noticed that in both scenarios I didn't experience my own death. Is that normal?"

"Not necessarily. Some people pull themselves out of a regression just before they die, others want to see what happens during and after the death process. Since both of your deaths were so horrible, your guides may have intentionally moved the virtual camera from your hands to his at the end. Also, your being able to see from his point of view is another indication of how strong the bond is between the two of you. What happens to one is felt by the other."

Something else that was different from the first session, Leilani felt alert and energized on her way home. Before going to bed, she listened to the tape of her life as Hannah and, even though she was fully conscious, still felt every emotion as though it was happening in present time.

She was also able to identify two others whose present incarnations were in her immediate field—Ruth was Edie Foster and Barnabas was Randy Krupp. At least now she knew why he gave her such an eerie feeling.

Again, the man's dilemma pushed all other dreams out of the way, but at least now the images were clearer and the overall picture had expanded.

The man is pacing back and forth...glancing at the calendar, looking at his watch...both he and the sparsely furnished room are detailed and in color...there's a window...boards on the outside conceal the view...he leans down and looks through a crack...outside is deep snow, a rock formation rises in the distance...like a two-headed smoke stack...a large buffalo comes into view...turns his massive head toward the window...a tear flows from its eye...the man looks at her... "They figure they'll take out thousands, maybe tens of thousands...they don't care about the children. There's nothing I can do by myself."

She asks him how she can help...

* * * * *

Joseph Grayson awoke with a jolt. He would have sworn she was there, in the room, talking to him. Once again he had dreamed of the beautiful Polynesian woman. This time, however, he had been able to see her face so clearly he was certain he would recognize her if she passed him on the street. Each time he dreamed of her, a little something had been added.

The one constant was that it seemed that she was trying to find him, which probably meant that she was a fellow agent. More than likely he had seen her at some point in the line of duty and his subconscious must have held onto the memory of her face, even if he had consciously forgotten it. Although, in truth, it would be very unusual for him to forget a face like that.

As far as he was aware, only one person, his superior officer, knew all the details of his assignment and where he had originally gone. That was over a year ago and he was now far from that town...or rather, he was fairly sure he was. The fact was, he had been locked in the back of a commercial truck for about thirty hours when they relocated this last time. Based on the driving time and amount of snow on the ground when they arrived, he assumed he was somewhere in the northern United States or southern Canada.

When he had initially infiltrated the small group of extremists, they were living in a farmhouse in Georgia. From there, they moved into a converted underground cavern in Kentucky, where they connected with a considerable number of hardcore secessionists. In the months that followed, there was a lot of traveling and both additions and deletions from the original membership. Just before the last move, they had joined up with another, much more organized and much more dangerous group of over a hundred men based in southeastern Texas.

By that time, Joseph had accomplished part of his original assignment. He had confirmed that the small band of men in Georgia was just one organ of a shape-shifting body connected by an internet website. He was also convinced that the body was growing steadily, with the Georgians representing the heart and the Texans being the muscle. He had yet to encounter the brain.

Along the way, the original, relatively impossible goal of creating a self-sufficient community that would secede from the United States government had become a mission to establish themselves as a power to be reckoned with. By the time the truck left Texas, he had been selected as part of a team of twenty-five men who would carry out a deadly attack. They intended to send a loud message to the politicians whose decisions were swiftly destroying all that made this country the best in the world.

Their current base of operations, wherever they were, appeared to be very isolated. The multi-building compound was surrounded by an endless view of deep snow, which created a natural security barrier. No one could arrive or depart without being noticed.

The main house was huge and outfitted as a dormitory, with all the basic necessities and comforts of survival. An adjacent storehouse was stocked with enough food and supplies to last a very long time.

And enough weapons to ward off a ground attack if threatened.

Joseph had been unable to learn who the compound belonged to. But there was no question that someone was financing this operation as well as the dissemination of the group's principles.

Being under deep cover often meant isolation and disappearing for long periods of time. Usually, however, when he had something vital to report, he could find a way to get himself, or at least the information, out. This time, he had been in a total lockdown phase for months.

To complicate the situation further, there were no phones or radios anywhere in the compound. All communication with the outside world was in the form of one computer with an internet access card and daily changing passwords. And that computer was in the very protective custody of a squirrelly little man known only as Skip. He had practically wrecked his cover to find out that little morsel.

Unfortunately, if Joseph did not figure something out soon, all the time and sacrifices will have been a waste. In fifteen days, he would probably be dead and so would a hell of a lot of people who had no idea how close Armageddon was.

Only his dreams gave him a shred of hope. Occasionally, in the past, he had a dream that later came true, so he had reason to believe there might actually be someone out there looking for him.

Joseph had never given much credence to praying in the past, but he had been doing a lot of it lately...especially to the black-haired beauty who came to him in his sleep.

* * * * *

Before going into the store Saturday, Leilani sent Rainy an email to thank her for the suggestion that she try regression therapy. She let her know when she'd be online Sunday morning if she had time to chat again. The next half hour was spent skimming various sites about the Puritans and Salem Village. This time she was barely surprised when she got to the witchcraft trials and found the names Reverend Parris, Mary Easty, Bridget Bishop, Susannah Sheldon and more. There was no reference to Hannah's accusation and hanging, but since she had not been legally tried, that made sense.

Satisfied that she hadn't made up all the details of that lifetime, she moved on to surfing for anything relevant to the clues she now had as to where the man might be.

The scene out of the man's window suggested he was somewhere with lots of snow, a tall rock and a buffalo. If she was meant to interpret the meanings of the images, based on her dream journal glossary, nothing logical came to her. Combinations of the words that the images could represent resulted in an infinite number of possible locations. Was he where the buffalo roam or Buffalo, New York? Either could have plenty of snow at this time of year, but how did the rock fit in? If all three were literally within his view, that eliminated a lot of places on the planet. It also left a vast area of the United States and Canada where he might be.

For the last few nights the mystery man had pushed aside all other dreams…except the one in which people were celebrating. For that reason, she was fairly certain that it was somehow connected to the other dreams about the man. Thus, March 10 might be a holiday on which there would be a parade. The glimpse of revelers made her think of Mardi Gras in New Orleans or Rio Carnival in Brazil.

Last night, the man had said, *"They figure they'll take out thousands, maybe tens of thousands…"* If a terrorist attack was planned for such an event, that could certainly be the outcome. Quickly she searched the date, but was further frustrated when she saw that there were all sorts of holidays all over the world on March 10.

The only positive result from her search was the physical sensation that she was on the right track.

Eventually she gave up and made another appointment with Phyllis for that evening.

Because the store was always busy on Saturdays, Leilani and Tillie would both work all day and close together at five.

"You look terrible," Tillie declared as soon as she saw Leilani. "You are obviously not getting any sleep. Have you eaten?"

Leilani gave her a quick hug. "I can always count on you to build my self-esteem. I assure you I have eaten more than I'm burning off. But the dream man mystery is driving me crazy."

"I've seen you disturbed by a dream before, but this one does seem to be having more of a lasting effect. Are you sure the problem's not just that hippie-therapy you've been trying?" The face Tillie made revealed her skepticism.

Leilani laughed. "It's *hypno*therapy, and actually it's beginning to help, but knowing that there's a deadline involved isn't helping my sleep time. I'm going for another session tonight."

"Hmph. Well, for your sake, I hope this one does it. You spend little enough time in the real world as it is." Tillie glanced out the front window of the store. "Speaking of the real world, your admirer is back again."

Leilani turned in time to see Randy Krupp opening the door. Instantly she had a flash of him as Barnabas and her stomach churned. At least now she realized that it was a hangover memory from their previous lives rather than there being anything dangerous about Mr. Krupp. He was clearly a very sweet, shy man. Because of their past relationship, however, she knew subtlety and avoidance was not the best way to deal with him.

She leaned close to Tillie and whispered, "Call Sally Wagner and tell her to get in here fast if she's still looking to meet a nice man. I'll make sure he sticks around 'til she gets here."

Tillie narrowed her eyes. "Aren't you the lady who hates setups?"

"Just make the call then I'll tell you a fascinating story."

As usual, Randy browsed for a while before he worked up his courage to approach Leilani. Out of the corner of her eye, she watched him take a hit on his inhaler and stride purposefully toward where she was helping a customer select a book. She could see that nothing was going to stop him today, so she didn't try. As soon as the other customer was satisfied, she greeted him.

"Hello again. How did the little bear go over?"

"Huh? Oh yes, the bear. Uh, very well. Really. It was a great idea. I really appreciated it. In fact, I was thinking that, um, maybe I could repay you by, um, taking you to lunch today...or...whenever?"

Leilani saw Sally Wagner walking into the shop and inwardly relaxed. "Oh thank you. That is very nice, but it's really not necessary. Besides, I'm afraid I have a boyfriend who would not be terribly understanding about my having lunch with such a handsome man." His disappointment was palpable, despite the compliment. "However, I'm really glad you happened to come in today. Do you see that pretty blonde lady talking to Tillie?"

He had to force himself to look. "Yes."

She lowered her voice and put her hand next to her mouth to pass on her big secret. "She was here when you were last week." Leilani paused to make sure he was paying attention. "She asked about you."

It still took him a few seconds to get it, but when he finally did, his response was somewhat positive. "Really? What was she asking?"

"Whether you were single, for one thing. You both like to read mysteries. May I introduce you?" She felt his attention slowly shift away from her and toward Sally.

"Uh, no thank you. I can take it from here."

"Good for you," Leilani said with a genuine smile as he walked away. It felt great to know that, in this case, history would *not* be repeating itself.

She and Tillie were too busy to chat until they locked the door behind the last customer.

"Whew!" Tillie said, with an exaggerated forehead swipe. "I didn't even get a chance to tell you how slick that Randy-Sally setup was. You better be careful or somebody might think you have a romantic streak!"

Leilani lifted her chin defensively. "I happen to be very romantic. I just keep it well hidden. Or maybe I just haven't met the right man yet."

"And you won't as long as you spend all your time thinking about a guy you only see in your dreams."

"I'll have you know that *guy* and I had quite a romantic relationship once upon a time. Believe me, after last night's regression, rescuing him wasn't the only thing I wanted to do!"

"Oooh, that was almost a naughty thought," Tillie said, lightly patting her chest. "Maybe I should rethink this hypno stuff and make an appointment myself. Seriously though, what will you do when you find him?"

The question made Leilani frown. She hadn't wanted to think about that. "I...I have no idea. In fact, I never gave that a thought. I mean, I was only thinking of doing what I usually do...pass the information on to someone else."

"Don't be ridiculous. You positively *must* meet him face-to-face. You told me that the two of you have some sort of strong bond. The chemistry would probably knock your socks off—something you desperately need, whether you'll admit it or not. You *have* to meet him in person!"

"If I ever find him."

"That was the fastest jump from optimism to pessimism that I've ever seen you do. Sounds like it's time to—" Tillie made the sound of a trumpet announcement. "Talk it through, baby."

Leilani chuckled but figured it was worth a try. She took a few minutes to relate the conclusions she'd come to that morning. However, nothing new came to her as she talked.

"I never pretend to understand how your dreams work, but there's one thing about this that doesn't make sense. If he really wants you to find him and he's able to tell you people are going to die, why doesn't he just tell you where he is?"

"Because he doesn't know." Leilani surprised herself with that answer. "Oh my. I didn't realize that until this second. It just popped into my head." *Thanks again, Grandma.* "He can't tell me where to find him because he has no idea where he is."

"So what does that mean?" Tillie said to keep her going.

"That I was right about a thought I had the other day. That he's probably a prisoner of war or kidnapping victim, which means that someone in authority must know he's missing. If I can just get a little more information about him, maybe Neil will be able to help figure it out. He must have overheard his captors talking about their plans...and that could mean that they were speaking English, which could be helpful in figuring out where he is." She gave Tillie a hug. "Thank you. You did it again. I feel much better."

"Good. Now I really have to go. Harvey's taking me out to dinner tonight."

Leilani arched an eyebrow. "Harvey? Again? Didn't you say something about the hair in his ears being a turn-off?"

Tillie waved a hand at her. "Oh that. I decided not to notice. Sometimes I forget how old I am and that I don't have many choices left. You should keep that in mind, sweetie."

Rather than set off down one of their well-tread conversational paths, Leilani bid Tillie good night and headed to her car. Despite the unhappy endings of the first two journeys with Phyllis, she was quite anxious to find out where tonight's session would take her.

* * * * *

"Imagine that you are looking in a mirror. Tell me what you see."

"A simple Irish woman…of a child-bearin' age." A hint of brogue slipped through. "That's what the advertisement said."

"What is your name?"

"Meg Kearney." She sighed and corrected herself in a resigned tone. "Mrs. Robert O'Donnell."

"Where are you now, Meg?"

"In my husband's bedroom. In the main house."

"And where is that house?"

"The O'Donnell Ranch. In the Wyoming Territory."

"And what about the man from your dream? Does he live there too?"

Before she could respond, the back of a beefy hand met her cheek with such force she was knocked to the floor.

Chapter Nine
Wyoming Territory, 1880

Robert O'Donnell backhanded his wife so hard she fell off the bed. *"You worthless whore!* I was ready and you ruined it again. You haven't done a single thing right since I brought you here. Get the hell out of my sight before I give you the beating you deserve!"

Meg quickly yanked the flannel nightgown back down over her hips and hurried out of his bedroom. She swiped at the tears on her cheeks as she ran to her own room and closed the door. Dropping onto the bed, she hugged her knees to her chest.

Robert O'Donnell was her husband. He had paid for her to perform all the services of a devoted wife. She should not feel violated by what just happened. With a sigh full of despair, she extinguished the bedside lamp and crawled under the covers.

It had been more than two years since Meg answered the advertisement in the newspaper for a mail-order bride. At the time she was working in New York's garment district, barely surviving on the low wages she was being paid. The long hours, hard work and poor diet had her looking forty instead of the twenty she really was.

For years before she saw the ad, Meg had been having dreams of a strikingly handsome man who took her into his arms and cherished her above all else. The instant she saw the ad, she felt a trembling in her stomach and knew that fate was calling on her to take a chance and head west. O'Donnell claimed to be a wealthy cattle rancher in the Wyoming Territory. He was looking for a young, healthy Irish girl to bear him an heir. She had heard wonderful tales of the opportunities for a new life available in the west. The idea of leaving behind the congestion and smoke-filled air of New York for the wide-open spaces was irresistible. Besides, she was more than ready to settle down and start a family…especially with a man like the one she saw in her dreams.

Her first pang of disappointment came when she arrived in Cheyenne and was met by her soon-to-be husband. Nearing sixty, Robert was not the man she had been dreaming about, but she had already accepted his offer. She needed to believe fate brought her here for a good reason. On the other hand she was everything Robert had been hoping for. They were married before they left town.

Meg soon discovered why he had chosen to look for a mail-order bride. He drank to excess on a nightly basis, something that made his sour daytime disposition even worse. There were no young women in the area willing to accept him as a husband. Added to that, O'Donnell needed someone who couldn't easily walk away from the never-ending chores required of a rancher's wife. Meg fit that requirement perfectly. She had no family to turn to and no funds of her own with which to start a new life elsewhere. To make matters worse, he had a physical impairment that had prevented him from consummating their marriage.

Unfortunately, he was not willing to stop trying and constantly blamed her for his failure.

The next morning, as usual, she was up before the sun rose to make breakfast for her husband and the ranch hands. As she'd learned her first week there, if she wasn't two steps ahead of Robert, he was more than eager to punish her. It didn't matter if there were others around or not because, as she also learned, none of the other men dared to interfere in the business between a husband and wife, especially when the husband was their boss.

Meg was halfway through putting the food on the table as several of the men walked in through the kitchen door. She watched as their boots tracked dirt from outside onto her clean floor and knew what her next chore would be.

"Good mornin', Mrs. O'Donnell. Everything smells really good," Jerry said as he sat down. He was the youngest, as well as the newest, of her husband's hired hands, brought on to take care of the horses.

As more men joined them at the table, Jerry continued, "Ya know, ma'am, my mama used to make me breakfast every mornin' and I thought it was the best darn cookin' in the world. But compared to your breakfast, it cain't hold a candle to it."

Meg laughed as he took a mouthful of food. "Jerry, you say the same thing every morning. I'm beginning to think that you just want more than your share of food."

Jerry's eyes went wide and, with sincerity, he said, "Oh no, ma'am! I wouldn't lie to you. It's the best darn cookin' in the world. I swear it."

As Robert walked into the kitchen he overheard the praise and grumbled, "You better watch the way you keep flattering my wife, kid. I'm not likely to let it again. Besides, the cooking is much better in town."

"Yes sir," Jerry said as he hurriedly cleaned his plate and rose from the table. "Thank you for breakfast, ma'am."

Meg cleared the table of dirty dishes and began washing them as the rest of the men filed out of the kitchen. Following them, Robert shot Meg one last look of contempt and let the door slam shut behind him.

Meg recoiled at the loud noise and tried to remember what it was like to *not* jump at the slightest sound. She took a deep breath and finished washing the dishes. Turning her attention to the dirt that had been tracked into the kitchen, she decided that cleaning it could wait. She needed to get out of the house while she had the chance. It had been a mild winter and the last of the snow was already melting under a clear sky and bright sun. The day was simply too beautiful to spend it locked up inside.

Anticipating an hour of freedom, Meg ran to her room to change from her long woolen dress into riding britches and a flannel shirt. A few minutes later, she grabbed her hat and coat and raced out the door.

When she reached the stables, Jerry was cleaning out the stalls. "Hi, Jerry," Meg said quietly so as not to startle him.

"Oh…hello ma'am. I didn't know you were wantin' to go ridin' today. I would've had Starlight ready to go for ya," he said.

"I just need to get away for a while. Would you mind getting her saddled up?" Meg asked as she stroked the white star on her mare's forehead.

"Anything for you, ma'am."

Meg ran her fingers through Starlight's white mane. "Good morning, pretty girl. Has Jerry been spoiling you today?"

Starlight snorted and turned her head to the bag of carrots sitting on the shelf.

"Oh, you haven't had your treat yet today, huh?"

The horse shook her head back and forth.

"Ah-ha." Meg paused as if to ponder the situation. "Well, have you been a good girl?"

She nodded her head up and down and stomped her hoof.

"In that case, I think if you ask Jerry nicely, he might be willing to give you your treat."

Starlight shifted herself toward Jerry and nuzzled her nose against him.

Jerry laughed and said, "All right, I guess you can have one piece." When Starlight snorted, he gave in. "Okay, okay. Two pieces, but that's it for now."

She neighed with delight and both Meg and Jerry laughed at her.

As he fed Starlight her treats, Meg asked, "So how are you doing, Jerry? I know Mr. O'Donnell can be demanding." Jerry was the only one on the ranch who spoke more than a few words to her and she hoped he would stick around a while.

"Yes, he can be, but he gave me a chance when nobody else would. I love horses. Ever since I was a youngin' I took care of my family's horses. It makes me happy. Besides, I don't have to work alongside him." He paused a moment then continued, "I just have to remember to hold my tongue when he's around, that's all."

Meg watched him fidget with the horse's bridle for a moment then asked, "Is there something bothering you, Jerry?"

He bit his lower lip as if trying to decide whether or not to tell her what was on his mind. "Well, um, I know it ain't my place or nothin', ma'am, but…well…"

"Whatever it is, you can tell me."

Scratching the top of his head, Jerry answered, "It's just that…well…that man don't treat ya right. You're a real nice lady and deserve to be treated better. My pa always told me that it takes a real man to treat a woman like a lady, and he treated my ma like she was a queen."

Knowing she had to change the subject, Meg helped him pull the bridle over her mare's head and asked, "You miss them, don't you?"

"Very much, but it was time for me to go out and make my own way in the world."

"I'm sure they're very proud of you." Meg tucked her long, curly red hair up under her hat and pulled its string tight beneath her chin.

As soon as she was out of the stable, she took off at a gallop. The only time she felt at peace in this place was when she was riding. Robert had presented her with the beautiful golden palomino as her wedding gift and taught her how to ride. It was the last nice thing he did for her.

Meg and Starlight both reveled in the feeling of the warm sunlight. For a while, the mare ran flat out. Meg flipped her hat back and let the wind whip through her hair, uncaring that her fair skin would probably burn and freckle. In fact, for the moment, she didn't have a care in the world.

When they neared their usual resting point, Starlight slowed to a walk.

Meg leaned down and hugged her mare's neck. "Thanks girl, I needed that."

Starlight snorted as if in protest.

Meg laughed. "Oh come on, you know you had fun."

Starlight whinnied and nodded her head up and down, making Meg laugh even harder.

Never in a million years would she have imagined that her best friend would be a horse, but here she was talking to the animal as though it were human. "I had another dream about him last night."

Starlight pricked up her ears to listen.

"He was handsome and sweet and sensitive and…he took me away from here on a great black stallion."

Starlight pranced at this bit of information.

"Oh, you'd like that? Well, I guess we could both do with some good lovin'." Meg giggled at her own silliness. "Let's go get you some water."

The O'Donnell Ranch was so large it could take a person several days to ride along its perimeters. Therefore, it was no wonder she had been able to find a private spot of her own. It was just one of many watering holes, but this one was completely hidden by trees. Meg would never have found it if Starlight hadn't taken her there to get a drink.

As she entered her small sanctuary, Meg let go of the life she led as Mrs. Robert O'Donnell and turned back the clock to when she was still Meg Kearney, a young girl with a head full of dreams.

Jerry had thoughtfully tied a blanket to the back of the saddle in case she got cold, but Meg had other plans for it. Knowing Starlight would not wander away, she dismounted and spread the blanket on the ground. Several months from now she might be tempted to strip down to her drawers and play in the water. However, today she would have to be satisfied with tossing stones and watching the ripples.

After a few minutes she saw Starlight's eyes droop closed and decided she could afford a short nap herself.

As soon as she lay down and closed her eyes, images from the dream she'd mentioned to Starlight danced through her mind. The man's long, jet black hair and amber eyes were unusual features. Yet she thought he was surely the most handsome man she had ever seen. Last night he had galloped toward her and scooped her up onto his huge black horse. The way he looked at her made her tremble with need. Though inexperienced, she knew this man was about to make her a real woman.

Meg felt a shadow fall over her and realized she must have dozed off. Assuming it was Starlight, she kept her eyes closed and said, "Give me a few more minutes, honey, and I promise we'll finish our ride."

"But, my love, I have waited so long already."

The deep, velvety sound startled her. She opened her eyes to find an Indian hovering over her.

"Oh my!" Meg jumped up to face the stranger and tried not to panic. "Please. Don't—" Meg's voice caught in her throat as her eyes focused on the face of the man standing before her. It was him. The man she had just been dreaming about. In flesh and blood. But he was an *Indian*! Somehow, she hadn't realized that in her dreams.

"I am sorry if I frightened you. I mean you no harm."

His English was perfect, not at all how she was told the savages spoke. Nor was he half naked. In fact, his clothing was no different from that worn by the men on the ranch. She had heard stories about Indians before, but the only thing that seemed scary about this man was how incredibly charming his smile was. She couldn't help but admire the square line of his jaw and prominent cheekbones.

Suddenly, Meg realized he had asked her a question while she was gaping at him. "I'm sorry, what did you say?"

His eyes sparkled with amusement. "I said, I was told I might find work on this ranch. My horse needed some water and led me here. I certainly did not mean to intrude."

Meg glanced over to where she had last seen Starlight and saw her rubbing noses with a great black mustang that stood at least three hands higher than her mare. "Oh, well in that case, I suppose I should welcome you to the O'Donnell Ranch." Meg extended her hand and said, "I'm Mrs. O'Donnell."

Taking her hand in his, he responded, "My name is Joseph Blackhawk." Without releasing her hand, he added, "I had not expected you to have a husband."

She was confused by his statement but distracted by the odd sensation of heat running up her arm from where their hands were joined. "I beg your pardon?"

"I had thought you would be...never mind, it is not important." He released her hand and took a step back from her. He was no longer smiling. "Could you direct me to where I might find your foreman?"

She felt as though she had slipped back into her dream world as she gave him directions and watched him ride away. None of it seemed real. She looked around the area and saw nothing to confirm that the encounter had truly occurred.

Had I still been dreaming? Or had the man from my dreams actually come to life? What had he meant about not expecting me to have a husband? Why had he looked at me as though we have known each other intimately? Why do I feel as though I have known him my whole life?

The only thing she was certain of was that it was well past time for her to return to the house.

Starlight picked up on her urgency and practically flew home. Meg was torn between completely blocking out the strange meeting and reviewing every second of it. Through most of her life, she'd had dreams that sometimes seemed more real than her real life. On more than a few occasions, something she had dreamed about happened afterward. She had known she would take a trip across the ocean, long before the actual journey occurred. She had known her father would be trampled by a horse and die. On the other hand, although she had seen the black-haired man hundreds of times in her dreams, she had begun to believe he was nothing more than that...a lovely dream.

It wasn't until she was preparing the evening meal that she realized he hadn't just looked at her intimately, he had spoken to her with familiarity as well. What was it he said? *"But, my love, I have waited so long already."* Was he flirting or, like her, had he seen her in his dreams? The sound of hungry men approaching the kitchen took precedence over figuring out an answer to those questions.

Normally on a ranch of this size, a cook would have been hired to prepare all the meals. However, because she had been unable to produce an heir, Robert decided she would earn her keep in another way. Therefore, she spent most of her days in the kitchen. She cooked, she served, she cleaned up and she cooked again, all the while remaining nearly invisible.

"You tell them," O'Donnell instructed his foreman.

Landy swallowed his food and made the announcement. "We took on a new man today. It's an injun."

The table grew silent as questioning glances ricocheted back and forth. Finally the oldest of the hands voiced what they were all thinking. "Thought this ranch was supposed to stay white. Never had no redskins here before. How do you know he won't kill us all in our sleep?"

"You know we been needin' somebody to break the new horses," Landy replied. "This man walked into the corral with one of the mares and had her calmed down in a couple minutes. We figure we'll test him out on Rocco tomorrow. Meanwhile, he'll eat and sleep in the stables, so if you don't bother him, he'll have no call to bother you."

"That reminds me," O'Donnell said, turning his head toward Meg. "When everyone's done here, take whatever's left over to the stables and leave it at the door. You'll be safe enough if you don't dally."

Meg could see the surprised looks on several of the men's faces and knew that they would never have sent one of their wives on such a dangerous mission. But she wasn't one of their wives. She belonged to a man who could barely stand the sight of her and probably wouldn't care if she was scalped in the process of doing his bidding.

As soon as all the men, including her husband, headed for the bunkhouse for their nightly card game, Meg prepared a plate for the new man. Rather than leave it at the door, however, she called out to him. "Mr. Blackhawk? Are you in here?"

He stepped out of the shadows without making a sound. "Hello again, Mrs. O'Donnell. I certainly didn't expect you to be the one to bring me dinner. I would have thought your husband would take precautions to keep you safe from the wild savage."

She wasn't sure how to respond to that, until she saw his grin. Returning his smile, she said, "Apparently, your skill with horses is worth more than my value as a wife."

As had happened earlier, a frown swiftly replaced his grin. "That would seem to say a lot about the foolishness of the man making that judgment."

Though she appreciated the comment, she simply shrugged. "If you need anything else—"

"I'll figure out how to manage myself. May I ask you a question?"

Up to that moment, she had avoided meeting his eyes, but his voice had suddenly changed. She raised her gaze and felt the breath catch in her chest as she saw the way he was looking at her. It felt as though he had thrown a lasso around her and was gently pulling her to him. She could barely manage to whisper a response. "Of course."

"Have you ever seen me before today?"

Her eyes widened with surprise. "Why…why would you ask me that?"

He tilted his head. "You did not answer my question."

"It's a silly question. You know we just met this morning."

"Then let me ask a different question. When you first saw me this morning, did you not feel as though you had seen me before?" When she remained silent, he continued, "I saw it clearly in your eyes. You *knew* me." He gave her a moment to acknowledge that before going on. "Just as I knew you."

Her mouth opened and closed twice before she could form a coherent thought. She was not ready to admit the truth quite yet. "What do you mean, you *knew* me? How could you know me? I was born in Ireland, lived in New York and have not left this ranch in two years. I am certain our paths have never crossed before, Mr. Blackhawk."

He took a step closer, enclosed her hand in his and asked, "Are you being honest or hiding the truth? Will you also deny that you felt something unusual when our hands touched — then or now?"

Meg closed her eyes as the tingling crawled up her arm and began to spread through her body. "I cannot deny that it is a most unusual feeling."

He reached for her other hand and held it firmly. "I saw you in a vision. It seemed impossible to me that a woman would have hair the color of fire itself, but then I saw you again in a dream last night. You came to me and we became one. And when I saw you this morning, you looked at me exactly as you had in the dream."

Only their hands were touching, and yet she felt their bodies melding together to become one, just as he said. "I have had dreams of you," she admitted hesitantly. "But there is nothing I can do about it. I am married to Robert."

"You don't love him."

"No. But I spoke the vows that ended my freedom to love anyone else." With those words, she eased her hands from his and turned back toward the house. She felt his fingers lightly touch her hair and she paused for one more moment.

"You speak more like a slave than a wife, and I do believe your President Lincoln abolished slavery some years ago."

"Good night, Mr. Blackhawk," she stated in a flat tone as she walked away.

"Good night, Meg."

Over the next several days Meg avoided going to the stables. She got Jerry to bring Joseph his meals and didn't even visit Starlight. The mere thought of another encounter with the Indian made her dizzy. She doubted that she could walk away from him a second time.

That didn't mean she couldn't watch him from a distance, however. He had captured the attention of everyone on the ranch with his remarkable abilities. Each day he spent hours in the corral working with the new horses. After his first time with the wild mustang Rocco, the cowboys stopped questioning Landy's decision to hire him on.

One morning, while he was training a mare, Meg could no longer be satisfied with watching him from inside the house. She hauled several carpets outside and hung them on a line for a good cleaning. Her ruse only worked for a few minutes. As she was peeking at Joseph from behind one of the rugs, he slowly turned and fixed his gaze on hers. The corner of his mouth turned up in a knowing grin. She felt the temperature in her body rise immediately and knew it had nothing to do with the sunshine.

She watched as he leaned close and whispered into the mare's ear. When the horse snorted in response, he stroked her chest and whispered again. This time the animal obeyed, rearing up on its hind legs as though waving at Meg. For that, Meg poked her head out a little farther and gave him a genuine smile of appreciation.

By that afternoon, she felt so guilty about ignoring Starlight that she quelled her nervousness and headed for the stables. Jerry and Joseph were working side by side. Jerry was combing Starlight's mane while Joseph was grooming his own stallion. The two horses were, once again, rubbing noses.

But what caused Meg to freeze in her tracks was the sight of Joseph without his shirt. She stood there mesmerized by the play of his back and shoulder muscles as he brushed his horse's coat. The beast's powerful form was a perfect match to his master's. Even Joseph's hair was tied back, almost imitating the horse's tail.

He stilled his hand for only a heartbeat and, instantly, she knew that he knew she was watching. Yet, as was proper, he did not acknowledge her presence.

"Oh, hello Mrs. O'Donnell," Jerry said brightly when he realized she was there. "I had a feelin' you'd be wantin' to take a ride this afternoon."

Joseph quietly donned his shirt but continued to keep his gaze averted.

"Have you met Mr. Blackhawk yet?" Jerry asked Meg. "He's really somethin'. He got Rocco to take a bit today. Nobody thought that horse would ever be brought around."

Meg braced herself for the introduction. "Hello, Mr. Blackhawk. You have certainly impressed everyone around here."

Joseph continued his task without turning around. "Thank you, ma'am. I am glad to have the work."

Meg couldn't decide if she was relieved or frustrated by the lack of direct attention. Her only choice was to do what she had set out to do, and that was to take Starlight for a ride. A few minutes later, Jerry had her horse saddled up for her and she was off.

Although Meg was in need of a hard ride, Starlight had other ideas. Regardless of Meg's encouragement, the mare was determined to saunter. It was almost as if she had been reluctant to leave the stable today. "What's the matter, girl? Are you mad at me for ignoring you? I'm sorry about that, but you see, that man has me all twisted up inside and I don't know what to do about it."

Starlight whinnied softly and gave her head a shake.

"That's easy for you to say!" Meg retorted with a laugh. "I saw you flirting with that big black stallion. And I don't blame you one bit. That is one gorgeous male. But it's different for me. I've made a promise that I'm bound to keep."

Again the horse objected to her statement.

"I know. I know. We weren't married in a church, so in the eyes of God, I'm not truly wed. And my husband treats his horse better than he treats me...no offense, girl." *Besides that, in the eyes of God I am still a maiden — grounds for annulment even in a church-sanctioned marriage.* "Nevertheless, what can I do about any of it now?"

Starlight lowered her head and swung it slowly from side to side as she continued to plod along. Suddenly, the ground shook and a thundering of hooves sounded from behind them. An instant later, a black blur flew past them, frightening the wits out of Meg. But Starlight knew exactly what it was. Rearing up on her hind legs, she let out a loud whinny and burst forward after the blur. Meg held on for dear life as Starlight chased after the males who had captured both their hearts.

By the time they reached her sanctuary, all four were breathing heavily.

"So, he's as fast as he is beautiful," Meg said as they dismounted. "What's his name?"

"Wa Et Da Ya E Wus Hath."

Meg blinked. "I don't think I can say that. What does it mean?"

Joseph chuckled. "It's Arapaho for 'Black Horse'."

She smirked at him. "Very original. I thought all Indian names were things like *He who saw the first dove in the morning*."

"Then his name *is* original."

"How about I just call him Blacky?"

Joseph turned and whispered in his stallion's ear and all Meg could think of was how it would feel to change places with the horse.

"He has no objection, but he said you may only call him that if you call me Joseph."

Rather than waste time objecting to something so simple, she shrugged and changed the subject. "Did anyone see you following me?"

"Jerry is the only one who knew I left and I headed in the opposite direction. You know, he's a little in love with you."

"No...well, maybe a little, but I haven't encouraged him. He's mostly homesick."

He walked over, spread a blanket on a patch of dried grass and sat down. It took her a moment of mental wrangling, but when she finally joined him he asked, "And what about you, Meg? Are you homesick as well?"

His question was so unexpected she was unable to answer right away. "It's been so long, I rarely think of home anymore."

"Long ago, when I first saw you in my dreams, you were a child running over green hills. There were others with hair like yours."

Meg did not bother to question his statement. He had just satisfied her curiosity. He *had* been dreaming of her all these years, while she had dreamt of him. "Yes, that was my family. We were in Ireland, a country very far from here. As pretty as this land is, I have never seen anything to match those green hills."

"So why did you leave?"

"When I was twelve my father died and the farm was too much for my mother to keep up. A neighbor of ours had an uncle in New York who agreed to pay our passage across the ocean, if we agreed to work in his factory. We believed the stories we heard about the streets being paved in gold. We were all very excited."

"We?"

"I had two younger brothers. Twins. They both died of pneumonia on the ship. My mother lasted two years in the workhouse before she joined them."

Joseph bowed his head and murmured a few phrases in his own language that sounded like a prayer. "When did you come here?"

"About two years ago. I thought agreeing to marry a stranger would be better than dying the way my mother did."

"But why would you marry him when you knew you were meant to be with me?"

Meg gave up the pretense of not understanding how he would know that. "By the time I realized that the man I had crossed the country to wed was not the man in my dreams, it was too late. I had no way to return and no other way to survive here except as his wife."

"A mistake then, but one that can be corrected."

She frowned. "I would rather not be given hope where there is none." She straightened her spine and shook her head as though clearing the sad thought from her mind. "Enough of me. Tell me about *your* family."

"Not today." In one fluid movement he rose to his feet then reached for her hand. "Come, you must return."

Anticipating the sensation his touch instilled, she let him help her to her feet. "I confess to being very confused. When you touch me I have thoughts…thoughts I know are wrong. And yet I feel no guilt. When Robert first put his hands on me, I could barely stand it. I thought it was because I was innocent. As his lawful wife I should not feel ashamed, yet I do. I am still innocent and you are just as much a stranger to me as he was, but with you…it's different."

"You know I am no stranger. We have known one another before, and in this life we have spent a great deal of time together in our dreams. That is why it feels different. You and I *are* meant to be together. That is why it would feel wrong for any other man to touch you." He brought her hand up to his lips and placed a soft kiss on it. "But why do you say you are still innocent?"

She lowered her gaze and let him figure the answer out on his own.

Again, he said something in his own strange language, but she had a fair guess of what it meant. "That was also meant to be," he stated with absolute certainty. Tenderly, he stroked her hair and trailed his hands down her back and up her arms. "You are mine. You always have been. You always will be. Mine."

She looked up at him and parted her lips. Breathlessly, she waited as he cupped her face in his hands. And when he pressed his mouth to hers, she knew she was finally where she belonged.

She still felt his kiss hours later as she went about her chores. She was still in O'Donnell's house, still in a wretched marriage, still a slave to his demands. But deep inside her hidden heart, a seed of hope had been planted.

That evening, she was blessed by the fact that Robert was too drunk to bother with her and she was able to retire to her room early. For the first time in nearly two years, she had something wonderful to think about.

When she first moved into the ranch house, she had found a small hole at the bottom of a wall in her dressing area. It was just big enough to hide her diary. The leather-bound book held her secret hopes and dreams, tears and frustrations from the day she left Ireland through her journey west. After a short time at the O'Donnell ranch, however, she had nothing more to add. Until tonight.

She got out the book, turned to a blank page and began to write. She had no idea what would happen tomorrow, but tonight she was happy.

For the next several days her chores kept her too busy to ride, but from time to time she would see Joseph. He would send her a knowing look and her heart would swell with joy. Each morning when she went into the kitchen, she found something had been placed on the table that had not been there the night before—a twig with a new leaf bud, a black pebble, a feather—all from him and all more valuable to her than gold. She knew it was irrational, but it felt as though she was a young girl being courted.

Finally, another opportunity arose for her to take a ride at a time when Joseph could meet her. This time, she had the blanket spread and was already sitting when he arrived. The smile on his face when he saw her waiting for him melted the last of the reservations she felt about sneaking away.

He sat down cross-legged in front of her and took both her hands in his. "I have thought of little else but touching you since we were last here."

She felt her cheeks flush and shyly lowered her gaze. "I as well."

He placed a finger beneath her chin and nudged her gaze back up to him. "Does that mean you would welcome another kiss?"

She managed to nod once before he leaned forward and touched his mouth to hers. That first gentle contact only seduced her to want more. The soft sigh that escaped her lips was all the permission he needed to give her the kind of kiss he truly wanted to. As his mouth closed firmly over hers, he shifted their bodies so that she was lying within his embrace.

She had never been held this way, with every inch of her body pressed to his, nor had she ever been kissed in a way that was both loving and hungry at the same time. Every shred of worry or judgment of right or wrong disintegrated as their hands and mouths aroused feelings only before experienced in their dreams.

After a few minutes he stilled her hands and withdrew slightly. "I love you, Meg. I have loved you since I was a boy. But I do not wish to have you do anything you are not ready for." He turned her in his arms so that her head was resting on his chest and felt her breathing slowly calm.

"Tell me about when you were a boy. Although I feel I have known you my entire life, I know so little about you."

"To tell you enough for you to understand about my people would take more time than we have today."

"Then just tell me one thing today and another tomorrow. How is it that you speak English so well?"

"When I was ten, I was taken in by missionaries. They taught me to read and write."

"Missionaries? What happened to your parents?"

Joseph's expression grew solemn. "They were killed."

"Oh, I'm so sorry. But didn't you have relatives? I'm not familiar with your customs, but weren't you raised in a tribe?"

He sighed. "This is not a happy story. Perhaps it should wait."

"I told you my unhappy story already." She placed a hand over his heart and said, "I have a feeling this is something I should know in order to understand the man I love."

It took him a moment to find a beginning point. "My people had grown tired of fighting the white man. Our chief—in English he was called Black Kettle—brought us to Fort Lyon to negotiate a settlement. The government promised us peace. On the way home, we were camped at Sand Creek when our chief sent our warriors out to hunt. While they were gone, Union soldiers attacked the camp. It was a massacre. They not only killed my parents but hundreds of other Arapaho and Cheyenne as well. I was one of the few children left alive."

She felt her heart constrict. "That is so horrible. I cannot even imagine such a thing."

He kissed her forehead. "You do not need to imagine it. You lost your family as well. Now let that be the end of unhappy stories." He raised her head and kissed her softly. "We must get back now, but tomorrow it is expected that I will be taking Rocco for a long ride. I will be here waiting for you, if you can manage it."

"I will find a way."

That night, Meg awoke from a nightmare so upsetting that she felt sick to her stomach. In her dream Joseph was kissing her, when suddenly a group of her husband's men broke them apart and dragged him off. Her dreams had come true too often for her to ignore such a loud warning. Something needed to be done to prevent another unhappy story.

The next day she saw Joseph ride off but could not get away unnoticed for several hours.

The instant she dismounted, they were in each other's arms. There was no need to speak as Joseph released her long enough to take the blankets from their horses, one to lie down on and the other to cover them with. Meg felt her conscience begin to question if she really wanted to take this step. However, as soon as he drew her down with him and resumed the magical kissing, passion again clouded her mind. She felt as though they had floated into a world all their own, where nothing but sensation mattered.

His lips placed sweet kisses on her eyes and nose, her chin and neck, and when he reached her ear he whispered a promise. "One day soon, it will be warm enough for me to see you unclothed, to let the sun witness how much I worship you. One day there will be no need to hurry. But for today, we cannot have everything as we would wish it to be. I had a dream last night. I was told that it is important that I make you mine as soon as possible. Do you understand?"

She felt no shyness as she looked deeply into his eyes. "Yes, Joseph. I had a similar dream. And I would be very happy if you would make me yours today."

His mouth crashed down on hers and she was momentarily surprised as he thrust his tongue forward to caress hers. His hands found sensitive flesh beneath her clothes and she felt herself grow wet with desire. It made her bold enough to explore his body as well. When her hand covered his manhood, his sharp intake of breath made her even bolder.

Even if their time had not been limited, neither of them had the patience to go slowly. They had both been waiting for this day for a very long time. Without care, buttons were undone and britches yanked down. She felt him pressing hard against her womanhood and braced herself for what was to come.

For a second, he held still and raised his head to look at her. "This will only hurt once, I promise. Next time, I will make it up to you."

"I'm ready. I want this. I want to be your woman."

Again his mouth came down hard on hers, distracting her for the heartbeat required for him to enter her body and tear through her virginal barrier.

The pain was minimal. She felt him move within her, groan and relax. It was hardly what she imagined, but he had promised that next time would be better and, somehow, she knew he would keep that promise. The pleasure of being joined with him in such a way was worth anything she needed to endure, now or ever again.

"Did I hurt you?"

"No. Not really."

He slowly eased almost entirely out of her body then pressed deep inside her again. "Did that hurt?"

She gasped as she felt him flex within her, touching some secret spot she had not known existed. "Oh my!" He repeated the movement and this time she moaned her appreciation.

"It is good now?"

"Oh dear God, yes," Meg said as she tilted her hips against his.

"You would like more?"

This time it was his turn to gasp as she clenched her muscles around him, proving that she was a quick learner.

"You will be sore if I continue," Joseph whispered hoarsely.

"I will be angry if you don't."

Not wanting to incur the wrath of a flame-haired woman, he continued the exquisite motion until every muscle in her body trembled with release.

Fortunately for Meg, Joseph retained some sense of clear-headedness and was able to help her get dressed and back on Starlight before too much more time had passed. After one last passionate kiss, he reluctantly sent her back to the house.

Jerry greeted her with a big smile when she entered the stables with Starlight. "That must have been some ride," he said cheerfully.

She blinked at him, suddenly aware she was grinning from ear to ear. "I...um...yes. We both enjoyed it very much." Not quite ready to give up the good feeling, she remained chatting with Jerry as he removed Starlight's saddle and brushed her down.

With her encouragement, Jerry told her one funny story after another about the mischief he and his brothers used to get into. Just as she burst out laughing, her husband appeared in the doorway looking huge and furious.

"What the hell is going on out here? What did I tell you about flirting with my wife, boy?" He marched straight toward Jerry, grabbed him by the shirt and tossed him several feet through the air, onto a stack of hay. "Pack up your things and be out of here by sundown!"

"Robert, no. He didn't—" A hard backhand against her cheek cut off the rest of her plea.

"Shut the hell up. You don't think I see what's going on here? With your face all flushed and your hair mussed up like a two-bit whore, you been leading him on. I've given you too much freedom for a woman. From now on, you ask permission to leave the house and you only go riding if me or Landy goes with you." With those words, he turned on his heel and strode out.

Meg rushed over to Jerry as he wiped away a tear. "I'm so sorry, Jerry. If I had thought for one minute—"

"*Meg!* Get in the house...*now!*"

As much as she wanted to console Jerry, she feared that lingering could make it worse for him. "I'm sorry," she said again and hurried to obey her husband.

That night she was awakened by a hand pressed over her mouth.

"Hush, love," Joseph whispered and replaced his hand with his mouth.

She would have loved nothing more than to give in to the feelings his kiss started, but the reality of their location was too much to ignore. She pressed hard against his chest and asked, "How did you get in here?"

"You left your window open."

When he tried to kiss her again, she pushed herself up in bed and backed away. Because of the dream she'd had, she felt absolutely terrified that something could happen to him. "You can't be here. Robert could come in any moment. He would kill you if he found you in here. He threw Jerry off the ranch today just for talking to me."

Calmly, Joseph lit the lamp by her bed. "O'Donnell is snoring loudly enough for us to hear him in the next county. Besides, I locked your door before waking you."

"He doesn't permit me to lock the door. Anyway, I'm sure he has a key."

"And by the time he finds that key, I'll be gone again. Now hush so that I can see your face." He held the lamp up beside her. "He struck you?"

She turned away. "It's nothing." He touched a finger to her bruised cheek, causing her to wince. She sighed and asked, "How did you know?"

"I heard the others talking. They say O'Donnell's temper could one day take your life. I cannot let that happen. You are my mate now and it is my vow to protect you. Would you prefer that I slit his throat in his sleep or challenge him in the daylight?"

Meg's eyes opened wide. "What? No! You can't do either one. Those men out there may not love him, but they are loyal to him. And though they respect what you do, you're still an Indian. If you kill him, they'll kill you. And if they kill you, I'll fight them, which will surely end my life as well. It's that simple. So I beg you, please do nothing that would cause you to be taken away from me." She clutched his shirt and shook him. "Swear it!"

He grasped her hands and held them. "Then we will leave here tonight."

"Dear Lord, no. Don't you see? He thinks of me as a possession. If you and I both disappeared, he would hunt us down. We would never have peace. There must be another way for us to be together."

Joseph took her in his arms and simply held her for the longest time before speaking. "I would rather kill him tonight." She stiffened and he hushed her again. "But I will not. He has offered me additional pay to help with the cattle drive in six weeks. If I go, there would be no question about my leaving his employ afterward. I have some money saved. With that, I could buy a small spread, perhaps in Texas, where it is warmer."

She relaxed back against him. "That sounds wonderful."

"A few weeks after they return without me, you will be able to leave without anyone connecting us. Wait for a night when they have been drinking heavily and everyone is asleep, then you and Starlight ride east. I will be camped nearby, waiting to go with you the moment you get away. Don't take anything with you. I'll have all we need."

She leaned her head back and gazed at him in wonder. "Do you really believe we could do that?"

Rather than answer, he kissed her deeply, then slipped out the window into the night.

Over the next six weeks, Meg made sure she did nothing to rile her husband or attract his unwanted attention. Luckily, because he was busy getting ready for the cattle drive, he wanted nothing more at the end of the day than his liquor and an undisturbed night's sleep.

Joseph was able to come to her room a few times each week, whenever he was certain everyone was bedded down. He would hold her and they would kiss and talk about the future, but he would not make love to her in that house. He promised they would have time enough for that once they were both away from there.

By the time the men began the cattle drive to Cheyenne, Meg had no doubt that she and Joseph were going to have a beautiful life together.

She also had no doubt that she was pregnant with his child.

The second month of Meg's pregnancy was not an easy one, as she was sick most of the time. At least there was no one around to witness it. By the time O'Donnell and his hands returned to the ranch, the constant vomiting and fatigue had calmed down to constant queasiness and only occasional vomiting.

The cattle drive and sale had gone very well, which put O'Donnell in a very good mood. As expected, several other hands besides Joseph took their pay and left, so no one considered the Indian's departure noteworthy.

Now all she had to do was wait a few more weeks to start her new life.

The night of his return, Robert told Meg to go to his bed and wait for him, as he was certain his good fortune would help him exercise his husbandly rights. Meg begged him to postpone as she was ill and would not want to infect him. He could see with his own eyes that she was not in the best of health and let her be.

Two weeks later, he noted that she still did not look well and suggested that she may need some rest from her chores. However, when he and several of the hands saw her upchucking outside after breakfast, his consideration turned to ugly suspicion. Because the others thought such evidence of his wife's possible pregnancy was a happy event, he did not reveal his rage to them. He would never want them to know that he could not possibly be the father.

After all the men had turned in for the night, he marched into her bedroom. With no warning, he pulled back the covers and ripped open the top of her nightgown. "It's true!"

Still groggy from sleep, Meg tried to cover herself, but that only made him angrier. Grabbing her by the hair, he dragged her out of bed and threw her to the floor. "You ungrateful whore!" He kicked her in the stomach.

"*Nooooo!*" Meg screamed and tried to protect herself, only to receive a second kick to her hip. "Please don't do this!"

He grabbed her hair again and pulled her to her feet. "Why not? You think I don't know what this means?" He squeezed a swollen breast so hard she cried out again. "With your husband you can barely stand to do your duty, but you would take a young boy into your body? A body that I bought and paid for? A body that I *own*?" His free hand closed around her throat and slammed her head against the wall with such force she thought she heard something crack.

Just as she was about to pass out from lack of breath, Joseph charged into the bedroom, ramming O'Donnell with his full body weight. It was enough to shove the bigger man away from Meg, but not enough to knock him down. Joseph swung his fist at the man's face before he had a chance to regain his balance and O'Donnell instantly repaid him in kind.

Meg collapsed onto the floor, gasping for air, as she was helpless to do anything but watch the two men enter battle. Furniture cracked, glass broke, obscenities were hurled and faces were bloodied, but neither man appeared to be wavering.

To Meg's horror, the bedroom was suddenly filled with O'Donnell's men, drunk, armed and ready to join the fight. A moment later, one of them hit Joseph's head with the butt of his gun and Joseph went limp. She tried to cry out, but a sharp pain in her lower abdomen took her breath away.

"Take him away!" O'Donnell shouted. "I heard my wife scream and saw this injun in here trying to rape her. Look!" He pointed at Meg and they all turned to stare. "Cover yourself, woman!"

"What do you want us to do with him, Boss?" asked Landy.

"You know what they say about injuns. The only good ones are dead ones. Take him outside and string him up!"

"*No!*" Meg cried, but her voice could not be heard over the rowdy shouts of the men as they dragged Joseph out of the bedroom. It was happening exactly as it had in her dream. She had to do something to stop it. As she tried to pull herself to her feet, another sharp pain paralyzed her and a moment later blood ran down her thighs. She knew what this meant but could not stop to think about that now. Fighting cramps and the pain in her head, she managed to get O'Donnell's rifle, load it and head out the door after the men.

As she stumbled outside, she saw the group gathered beneath a large tree. Joseph was slumped forward on a horse with his hands tied behind his back, while Landy prepared a noose. They were only a few hundred feet away, but Meg's body was not cooperating.

She fired one shot into the air and screamed, "*Stop!*" Her order was so surprising, the men obeyed long enough for her to reload the gun and make it the rest of the way across the yard.

Determined to stop them no matter what it took, she pointed the rifle at her husband and demanded, "Let him down or I will shoot you."

"Don't be ridiculous, woman," Robert said with a sneer as she approached the lynch mob. "Put that gun down. It's just an injun."

Out of the corner of her eye she saw Joseph slowly raise his head and turn toward her. "Joseph, are you all right?"

Robert's eyes widened with awareness as his gaze flashed from his wife to the Indian and back to the blood on her gown. Without hesitation, he grabbed Landy's gun and fired two shots — one into Meg's chest and the other into Joseph's head.

Chapter Ten

Meg's entire body was racked with excruciating pain. Between the miscarriage and the gunshot to her chest, blood was pouring out of her. She felt her heartbeat weaken and knew it would be over soon.

"*Leilani*! Wake up! This is not happening to you. It happened to Meg. A long time ago. You must separate from Meg. *Now!*" Phyllis loudly clapped her hands.

Leilani heard the command and wanted to obey, yet it still took a monumental effort to leave Meg and return to her physical body. The moment she did, she burst into tears. Not a trickle like before, but gasping, heart-wrenching sobs that came from the core of her being.

As soon as she gathered some composure, her heartache continued to spill out in words. "Why would he do that…my beautiful Joseph…and…and…" She let out another heavy sob as she clutched her stomach. "My baby…I lost my baby."

Phyllis knelt down and gathered her in her arms. "It's okay. You're okay. And that baby will be back with you again."

"Will it? Are you sure?"

"I have a very strong feeling that she's just waiting for an invitation." Phyllis released her hold on Leilani and handed her the box of tissues.

Leilani wiped her wet cheeks and blew her nose. "Wow. I don't think I want to do this anymore."

"Good. Because I think you have more than enough to draw some useful conclusions. You need to stay here for a while longer, so why don't we go over what you've got." She handed her a glass of water and waited for her to drink it all before going on. "You said something earlier about how you figured he doesn't know exactly where he is, so he can't tell you that information. But in your dream he showed you what he saw out his window."

Leilani felt her conscious mind taking control again. "Snow, buffalo, rock. I didn't see any of that in this trip, but of the three places I've seen, Wyoming is the only one that could possibly match with the view out his window. Maybe I could find—" She started to rise but a wave of dizziness forced her to lie back on the pillows again.

"Give it a little more time," Phyllis instructed with a smile. "You can do the research when you get home. What I wanted you to realize is that something missing in the dream may have been supplied in the regression. You said that he never told you his name. Why do you think that is?"

Leilani closed her eyes for a moment and an answer came to her. "I get the sense that he thinks I know who he is, but there's also something else about his name..." She strained to hear another answer, but her connection to the Other Side had completely disintegrated. "It's gone."

"That's okay, maybe it will come to you in your dreams tonight. But meanwhile, I realized something in this session that could be relevant to his name. Consider this. In all three of the past lives you visited, his first name was Joseph."

Leilani nodded as understanding set in and she carefully drew herself up on the couch. "Joseph Whitely, Joseph Browning, Joseph Blackhawk. It isn't just that the first names were the same...the last names all had a color in it. That has to be another clue. Good. I feel like we're getting somewhere now. What else? What else? We already figured out from the first two that the karma had to do with my being killed and his not being able to save me."

"And in this one," Phyllis quickly continued, "he saved you from being beaten to death, only to put himself in jeopardy."

"Then I tried to save him, but we *both* ended up being killed."

"Add to that how your relationship progressed from childhood best friends to physical attraction to passionate lovers..."

"But all ended with tragic separation." Leilani sighed. "I come right back to the fact that we don't know each other at all in this lifetime. The strong connection just isn't here."

"Are you sure about that? In this last lifetime, he acknowledged an ability to dream the future. You've said that it seemed your dream man was talking directly to you. Maybe he's a lucid dreamer as well. Despite the fact that you two have not yet met in the physical world, you seem to have a pretty strong connection in the dream world. But let's get back to the other similarities. I think the *ways* you were killed are telling you something important as well."

Leilani tilted her head and frowned as she reviewed the material. "Let's see, I was hacked up and burned in the first."

"By?"

"By an angry mob of black slaves."

"Because?"

"I was...white."

"And the second?"

"I was hung."

"By?"

Leilani was about to say Barnabas, but he hadn't personally killed her. He had just set the wheels of injustice in motion. "By a frightened mob of narrow-minded Puritans."

"Because?"

"They thought I was a witch being empowered by Satan. Because I wasn't like them." It was all suddenly crystal clear. "And in the third, the angry mob hated Joseph because he was an Indian, and I was killed for allowing him to touch me."

Phyllis summarized the common elements. "Hatred, prejudice, mob mentality, mindless violence. These are ugly things that still thrive today. In my experience, the first of a series of regressions often holds the biggest key, even if it takes several more sessions to see it."

Leilani was now fully awake and grounded again. "And in this case, the first one involved a mass murder, not just one or two innocents. If I throw in the scene I saw with all the people and the parade, well, we could be looking at some kind of terrorist attack. Geez, Phyllis. I've got to tell you, I've never gotten information of this magnitude before."

"Not even before September 11? I vividly remember having a terrifying dream the night before that."

"Oh yes, of course. A lot of people did. But it was a precognition that played out within a few hours of my dreaming it. I didn't have any sense that I could do anything to prevent it. There's no question in my mind that I'm supposed to do something about this. But I still don't feel like I have enough to pass on."

"I have a feeling you will by tomorrow morning. You cemented the bond between the two of you tonight. That's undoubtedly going to have an effect on your dreamtime. My suggestion is that you go home, watch a meaningless sitcom or two and go to sleep. Don't listen to the tape tonight or do any research. Just let it process on its own."

Leilani rose to leave, but Phyllis had one more issue to discuss. "I don't know if you realize it at the moment, but when you listen to the tape, you're going to hear something that you might want to talk about. While you were under, you said you recognized who Robert O'Donnell is in this lifetime."

Leilani had a vague recollection of what she was talking about but she couldn't bring it forward. With a shrug, she asked, "Who did I say he is?"

"Your father."

"*What?* That's ridiculous. He's more like Hannah's father was. My father is one of the most loving, gentle men you could ever meet. He never did anything to hurt me or any other human being!"

"I'm very relieved to hear that. Which means you've now seen how a simple karmic balance can occur from one lifetime to another. His debt to you from that lifetime was repaid with kindness and protection in this one. The balance was achieved when he experienced the premature loss of his wife—"

"And allowed me to go live with my grandmother, even though he would miss me, because he knew that was the best place for me to grow. Yes, I can see how it was all part of a greater plan. I just wish balancing out the karma between me and my dream man was half as simple."

Chapter Eleven

"Good morning, sleepyhead."

Joseph felt his body instantly respond to her voice but pretended he didn't want to be bothered. He wanted to see what she might do to wake him up.

She placed her lips next to his ear and whispered, "I know you're faking. Little Joey already gave you away."

He groaned as though she was truly annoying him, then rolled onto his side and buried his head under the pillow.

"Okay, I accept your challenge."

He felt her slowly slide the sheet downward, baring his body to her gaze. It was a good thing he'd covered his head or she'd see him biting his lip. She made him wait several seconds to find out how she intended to torture him. Her weight shifted on the bed and he had his answer. She was hovering over him, letting her long black hair brush over his back, his arm, his chest. His nipples contracted instantly and he groaned again. He knew where she was heading, but she was going to take her good, sweet, sexy time getting there.

He only lasted another few seconds before he tossed the pillow across the room, flipped her onto her back and pinned her with his body. His grin grew wider as he noticed that his Polynesian princess was wearing nothing but the cocky smile of a winner. It didn't matter how often they'd done this, he couldn't wait another second to have her and he knew she would be ready for him. But she deserved a little return torture first.

Deliberately taking his time, he made love to each beautiful, dark-nippled breast before trailing kisses down over her stomach toward an even more sensitive area. She tried to be patient but gave in after only a few minutes. Drawing his mouth up to hers, she teased it with her tongue as he smoothly slid into her body.

There was always something extra special about morning sex with her, as though it was a guarantee of a perfect day ahead. This morning felt more like a leisurely stroll than a wild race to a finish line, but the pleasure was always incredible either way.

After making sure she had climaxed a second time, he asked, "Have I told you how much I love you yet today?"

She giggled and kissed him gently. "I think I got the message. Ready for coffee?"

He squeezed her perfectly rounded bottom. "I'll get the coffee. You get in the shower. You always take longer than I do."

"If that's another challenge, I accept. And I'll win too. I can't wait to get going today. We are going to have such a good time!"

It still took a while for them to get out of the house, but the joint shower had been worth the extra time.

They walked out their front door and were instantly in the middle of a crowd of happy people. The loud music had everyone dancing to the Latin beat. It took him a moment to figure out where he was, but the instant he did, panic struck him like a knife in his chest. He yanked on her hand. "We have to go. Come on."

She laughed at him. "No way. We just got here. This is going to be fun! Look! The parade is coming this way."

He tried to pull her away from the crowd but he lost his grip on her hand. He struggled and shoved and pushed to get to her but she was swallowed up by the mass of humanity.

An instant later, an explosion obliterated his world.

"Noooooo!"

* * * * *

Joseph Grayson was awakened by his own scream of rage. His heart was pounding and tears were running down his face. This wasn't the first time he'd had a realistic dream, but it was the first time he'd had one like this, where all his senses had been totally involved. It was as though he was truly *in* the dream rather than watching it.

He had been seeing the black-haired woman in his dreams for a week, but she had always been at a distance. And there was certainly no hint of an intimate relationship between them. He had no idea how he had made the leap from curious observer to full-out wet dream.

The other dreams had given him a sense that he had seen her somewhere before. This dream left no doubt about his knowing her, knowing every swell and curve of her body, knowing that she had an unlikely shade of blue eyes for a woman with otherwise Polynesian features, knowing how she needed her coffee to get moving in the morning, knowing how long it took her to take a shower. In this dream, he knew details about her that only a *husband* would know.

Even more bewildering, however, was the intense pain he was still feeling in his throat and chest. The sensation was unfamiliar to him personally, but his logical mind deduced that it was desolating heartbreak—a feeling that could only be the result of loving someone with every fiber of one's being then losing that person.

How odd.

There was absolutely no one in his past with whom he had ever had that kind of a connection. Nor did he ever wish for someone like that to come into his life. It definitely wouldn't fit in with the life he had chosen to lead. There had been a few women he liked a lot and a few more who had aroused his lust for longer than an hour, but the word "love" had never entered his mind, let alone come out of his mouth. Nothing in his relationship experience correlated with what he was feeling in the dream, yet it felt familiar with that woman. In fact, it felt perfectly...*normal.*

He knew, without a moment's hesitation, that if she was in his life, he would change everything else to keep her safely in his arms.

That thought caused his mind to jump to the end of the dream. She was there when the bombs went off, and he was unable to stop it or save her. That had to be an important clue to the dream's meaning. All the lovey-dovey stuff meant nothing compared to that.

He had already concluded that she was connected to the Bureau and actively looking for him. So perhaps, even though she had not located him, she had been able to figure out what was about to happen and where. It was quite possible that there was a team of agents already working to prevent the disaster.

Unfortunately, his dream suggested that they didn't figure it out in time. And because she was trying to help him, she would end up being one of the thousands of victims.

Again, he felt as though a fist clenched around his heart and for a moment he had trouble breathing. He had the distinct impression that if he failed to save her, his own life would lose all meaning. That made no sense whatsoever, yet he couldn't make the feeling go away with logic.

The worst part of it was that he was truly helpless to do anything about it, so what good did the dream warning do?

He had his answer the next instant. The dream had shown him what was missing in his life. It was rather ironic that he would get that bit of vital information so close to his death.

Chapter Twelve

The salsa music pulls her into the crowd...all around her people are laughing, dancing, shouting...children sitting atop their papis' shoulders...the brightly colored parade floats gliding by...pretty young people waving...banners with Spanish words...Cuba Libre...a street sign...Calle Ocho...the smell of spicy food wafts toward her...she turns to see what the vendor is selling from his cart...suddenly the cart explodes...the vendor's body torn apart...another explosion behind her...another across the street...a building demolished in an instant...glass shards, bricks and splintered wood become more weapons of death...blasts sound from blocks away in each direction...fires everywhere...screaming...panicked faces smeared with blood...body parts flying...children crying...everyone pushing, shoving, frantically trying to escape the hellish scene but every path is blocked by pieces of buildings and dead bodies...

It took superhuman effort to stay in bed and write down everything she saw in the terrifying dream. She needed to get online and confirm her suspicions. She needed to call Neil and get him working on this. She needed to figure out why she was in the crowd, rather than just watching the scene unfold, as she normally would. But first, it was vital that she write down every single thing before the images disintegrated.

As soon as her notes were transcribed into her journal she got online. Within minutes, she had her confirmation. The celebration in her dream was definitely the annual Carnaval Miami, which takes place along Eighth Street, also known as *Calle Ocho*, in Little Havana. It is touted as the largest street festival in the United States, with crowds regularly topping one hundred thousand, a large percentage of which are of Cuban descent. This year, one of the days of that celebration will be March 10 — the date circled on the man's calendar.

A glance at her own calendar increased her concern. Bloody Saturday was only two weeks away.

There was nothing else in her dreamtime about the man or his location. The only thing she felt certain of was that he was still alive. But what about his captors? Were they still with him in the place that could be Wyoming, or on their way to Miami to enact their heinous plans?

Who were the bad guys in this picture? Who hated Cubans enough to commit the mass murder she saw in her dream? When she thought of bigotry in general, several extremist groups came to mind immediately. However, she didn't get any strong feeling about any of them being behind this.

She set her questions aside and called Neil.

"Hey, pal. How ya doin'? I know I told Cal and Edie that you and I were working today but I didn't —"

"Do you know anybody connected with Carnaval Miami?"

"My God! I can't believe you asked that! I was going to call you later today about it. Edie's sister — remember, you met her at Christmas — called last night and invited us to go down and stay with them in Miami so that we could all go to the festival together. We thought you could join us —"

"*NO!*" Leilani shouted.

"Whoa, girl. I swear this wouldn't be any kind of setup. Only family."

"No! You can't go. Nobody can go. Something awful is going to happen there." The question as to why she had dreamed of being in the crowd had just been answered.

"Can we back up a little please?"

"Oh sorry. The dream is still haunting me. Let me give you the highlights. On March 10 a lot of bombs are going to explode along the parade route. Thousands of people will be killed, some by the bombs, some trapped and trampled, unless someone stops it. I'm pretty sure hate is at the root of their plan. It could even be that the group behind it is prejudiced against Cubans specifically. And there's a man. His name is probably Joseph, with a last name that has a color in it, like Whitely, Browning or Blackhawk. I think he's their captive, but he knows all about their plan. Oh and they might be in Wyoming."

Neil cleared his throat. "You know I trust your dreams and usually I get right on something you warn me about, but do you realize how uncertain you sounded about some of those pieces?"

She sighed. "Yes, I do. This whole thing has been different from anything I've dealt with before. But I am absolutely positive about something disastrous happening on *Calle Ocho* in Miami, on March 10, and you're the only one I know who can help me prevent it."

"Okay, I'll make some calls, but I would expect that security will be pretty high anyway."

"Make sure they have those special dogs that sniff out bombs."

"Yes, ma'am."

"And make sure no one from your family goes anywhere near Little Havana on the tenth. In fact, tell anybody you care about. And check if there's a missing person's report on a Joseph Something-with-a-color-in-it."

"Yes, ma'am," he repeated, with a distinct smile in his voice.

"I know that's a lot to ask, but I have a strong feeling that finding him, or something about him, could make all the difference."

* * * * *

"Hey, Vic, what's with you man? I asked you to pass the grits!"

"Sorry. Didn't get much sleep last night," he replied, quickly passing the bowl down the long table. Joseph Grayson mentally slapped himself in the forehead. He had been Vic to these guys for the last year and yet a moment ago he hadn't answered when called by that name.

"Yeah, we know," a big brute named Butch called from the other table. "We heard you yelling at somebody around four this morning."

"Sorry," he repeated and focused on his breakfast. From time to time he suffered from nightmares, not unusual for someone in his line of work. In his current living situation, however, it was such a risk that he'd been making an effort not to fall into a deep sleep, so he was tired all the time. On the other hand, the problem was so annoying to the others that he had ended up with a room to himself. It was just a storage room with a boarded-up window, but at least he was alone for a few hours every night. Being closed up in a house with twenty-four other men for the past two months had him appreciating every solitary moment he could get.

"You ever think about seein' a shrink about those nightmares?" Skip asked.

"What're they about anyway?" Butch interjected. "Is the devil after you or what?"

"As pretty as he is, it's probably just some faggot wantin' to get a little ass!" This bit of brilliance was offered by Ned, the most likely guy in the group to be a closet homosexual.

"Leave Vic alone," commanded Earl, the self-appointed captain of the band of incredibly unattractive men. "Every man has to deal with his own nightmares in his own way. For all you know, if you were in Vic's shoes, every one of you might be wakin' up screamin' in the middle of the night."

Joseph caught Earl's pointed speech and met his stare without flinching. Outwardly, he showed no sign of understanding what Earl might be hinting at, but inside his head he was replaying the conversation he had overheard a week ago. As he often did after everyone was asleep, he had been prowling around the enormous house when muffled voices had drawn him toward the kitchen. What they were saying kept him from revealing his presence...

"*How much can we trust the source?*" asked Earl.

"*It's not a hundred percent, if that's what you mean,*" replied Skip. "*But it's better than fifty. The FBI definitely assigned an agent to investigate us, right about the time Vic showed up. The description could be a match too.*"

Earl whistled. "*I still find it hard to believe. He fits in better than my own son. He's never done a single thing to make me doubt his loyalty. In fact, he's the one who came up with the suggestion to transport the troops and weapons using trucks made up to look like the vendors' delivery trucks.*"

"*Which could be the best way for him to be able to tell the Feds what to look for.*"

"*That's true. But he really seemed committed to everything we believe in. I've never been that wrong about somebody. He's been with us for a year now. Either he shares our opinions or he's one hell of an actor.*"

"*Well, like I said, there's a chance the information is wrong about him being the spy. It could be one of the others we've picked up.*"

"*Yeah, but we can't take that chance, can we? So what could the damage be if it's true? We know he hasn't been able to leave the compound because of the snow and there's no way he could have gotten a message out. Right?*"

"*Right,*" Skip assured him confidently. "*I've constantly scanned for electronic devices and radio signals. I've got the only computer and I never let the internet access card out of my sight. Unless he's figured out a way to reconfigure the DVD player, he hasn't gotten a message out. Even if he did, we used complete blackout precautions bringing everyone here, so he couldn't give our location away if he wanted to. But once we leave here next week, it could be a different story.*"

"*Just to make sure, we'll change some details and not fill him in.*"

"*Or I could just kill him,*" Earl Junior stated in a chilling tone.

For several seconds no one spoke then Earl gave his judgment. "No. Not yet anyway. If he is an agent, and something goes wrong while we're still here, he could have value as a bargaining chip."

"Or better yet," offered Skip, "we could always let him escape with some false information that would have them looking in the wrong place at the wrong time."

"Bad idea. Too much could go wrong," Earl stated. "It's not even worth the risk of taking him along with us now. If we don't need him to bargain with by the time we leave, Junior can have his way. For the moment though, this goes no further than the three of us. Everyone needs to keep treating him like he's one of the team and the best way to do that is make sure no one has reason to think otherwise. You got that, Junior?"

"Yeah. I got it." Those four words carried both annoyance that his father always spoke to him like a child and disappointment that he wouldn't get to kill anyone that night...

If he had not overheard that conversation, Joseph would not have noticed that anything had changed. Every day was dragging along just as it had been for the last two months.

Earl was smart—a bigot, a tyrant and a fanatic, but smart. Skip was more of a mystery. He wasn't just intelligent, he was dispassionate. Besides being Earl's right-hand man, he was the group's accountant, communications officer and computer geek. Joseph had a suspicion that Skip was not as devoted to the group's concept as he was to the power and money being generated by their movement.

Neither Earl nor Skip had said or done anything that might make it seem like they doubted Joseph's loyalty. Earl Junior, on the other hand, was constantly sizing him up now. His eyes gave away the fact that he was mentally murdering him in a number of ways. He was such a strange character to begin with that Joseph might not have given a second thought to the odd attention. Knowing that the young man would happily blow his brains out just for the fun of it kept Joseph more alert around him. The closer they got to their departure date with nothing threatening their plan, the more certain Joseph was that his days were numbered.

He let his gaze casually roam around the room. The rest of the guys were basically foot soldiers, all sitting around waiting for their marching orders. If anything was going on behind his back, he'd see it in a few of their faces. The only thing he saw was Ned, sneaking a peak at him then abruptly looking away when caught. Poor Ned. He was just as trapped and had just as little hope of being rescued as Joseph did.

Joseph didn't miss the fact that his living situation could easily have been at the root of his strange dream. The part about the bomb going off at Carnaval Miami was obvious since that was straight out of the actual plan of attack. But the part with the woman could have been triggered by his present circumstances as well.

Earl had a firm rule about no women being part of their group or visiting overnight. He really believed females were all manipulative Delilahs who drained men of their strength. He also compared their present situation to a team of football players preparing for the Super Bowl. Celibacy was required to keep their minds on the big game and maintain their testosterone at peak aggression levels. Joseph hadn't had sex with a woman in over six months. He hadn't even seen a female in the flesh in the last two, so it was no wonder he was dreaming about having sex with a beautiful woman.

As soon as he was done with breakfast, he headed for the workout room to burn off the remnants of the nightmare. However, he had the strangest feeling that no amount of weightlifting was going to make him forget how it felt to have his dream woman's body entwined with his own.

Chapter Thirteen

Salsa music...people laughing, dancing, shouting...children... parade floats...young people waving...banners with Spanish words...Cuba Libre...Calle Ocho...the smell of spicy food wafts toward her from a vendor's cart...the cart explodes...another explosion behind her...another across the street...a building demolished in an instant...fires everywhere...screaming...panicked faces smeared with blood...

The man is on his knees...hands tied behind his back...a group of men line up behind him, no faces are discernible...in unison they raise their right arms...a pistol in each hand...all pointed at the bound man's head...shots are fired...

When she awoke Monday morning, Leilani didn't need to glance at the notes on her nightstand to know what they said. Not only was the disaster still going to occur, her sense that the man was going to die was now confirmed.

Normally when she passed on a tip to Neil, she was immediately relieved of any responsibility. Unfortunately, nothing about her recent dreams was normal. Instead of being able to let go of the images after giving the information to Neil, the dream had worsened. He clearly had not been able to do anything with the information yet.

She forced herself to go through her regular morning routine. She made herself walk faster and expend more energy than usual. At the beach, she breathed the salt air more deeply, but none of it helped her get grounded. It felt as though her nerves were on the outside of her body. She was supposed to be doing something to help the man, that much she understood. If calling Neil wasn't enough, what else could she do?

One thing was certain. Going into the store this morning was not going to improve the situation. As soon as she got home, she called Tillie.

"I need to take a few days off," she told her friend. "I haven't figured out what I'll be doing, but I have a strong feeling that I need to have an open schedule."

"I don't like the sound of that," Tillie responded. "But I know better than to try to talk you out of it. Don't worry about the store. I'll take care of everything."

"I know you would, but I have a better idea. All I want you to do is go put a sign in the door that we're closed for the week then take a vacation. I'll feel better knowing you're not climbing any ladders or carrying boxes while I'm out."

Tillie laughed. "Just because I won't be in the store doesn't mean I won't be climbing ladders. With all this unexpected time on my hands, I might get an urge to clean my rain gutters."

"Don't you dare! Promise me you won't do anything this week that might give me more nightmares."

"I suppose that includes the bungee jump I had planned for tomorrow. You know, for a young woman, you can be terribly boring. Okay, I promise, no nightmare-inducing stunts."

Her next call was to Neil. "I know if you had anything you would've called me already, but I'm really stressed out over this."

"I can tell. You don't sound like yourself at all. You're right though. If I had anything important, I'd have called. But that's a good thing, really. I've contacted people on each of the police departments involved with the Carnaval. They haven't gotten a single tip suggesting that something might happen. They are very well prepared and will have plenty of uniformed and undercover officers on duty."

"What about the bomb-sniffing dogs?"

"I made the suggestion."

"But?"

He sighed. "They can walk a dog along the street before the crowd starts gathering but after that, well, it's just not possible."

"How about security checkpoints? Couldn't the dogs be there? And what about metal detectors for weapons?"

Neil's long hesitation was an answer in itself. "Look, pal. I don't want to get you more upset, but this isn't the kind of event that can be controlled like that. It's all outside, in the middle of a city. All along the parade route there are side roads and parking garages and buildings with multiple entrance and exit points. Besides the spectators, which could number in the six figures, there are thousands of people involved in the activities—"

"Like vendors with carts?" The image of the exploding cart and man flashed in her mind.

"Exactly. I'm afraid there's not much the police can do without having someone or something specific to look for."

She knew that even before he said it aloud. "Right. So the key is to stop these people before they get to the Carnaval."

"Well, yes, that would be the best way to prevent it from happening. But that's easier said than done."

"I can't leave it at that. Remember how I said it might be a group acting on prejudice or hate? The local police might not know anything about something being planned by that sort of group but—"

"The FBI would," Neil finished. "Okay. I have an acquaintance I could call. Her name's Gayle. She's a Special Agent and if I remember correctly, she's open-minded about psychic tips. I'll give her a call and tell her everything you told me. Keep your cell phone handy in case she wants to talk to you directly."

"You got it. Thank you *sooo* much!" Leilani felt the first little wave of relief ripple through her body. The FBI would know about a group like that. They might even know if a man named Joseph was being held by such a group. Besides that logical deduction, she also noted the confirming shiver she had when

Neil spoke the words "Special Agent". Those words were important to solving this mystery, that was for certain.

Her cell phone alarm beeped, letting her know it was time to chat with Rainy online. As briefly as possible, Leilani let her know how the regression therapy had worked and how much closer she was to analyzing the dreams about the man, thanks to her suggestion.

T: *Can I help with anything else?*

L: *Got any thoughts about how I can figure out exactly where he is?*

T: *What ya got so far?*

L: *Lotsa snow, a buffalo & a tall rock shaped like a double smokestack.*

T: *Hold on a sec while I pull some cards.*

Leilani stared at the blinking cursor on her monitor and hoped for a clear answer. She didn't get one.

T: *You already know where he is.*

L: *Huh?*

T: *Sorry. That's all I'm getting. Maybe you need to take another look at your dream notes and listen to the tapes again. The cards are saying your answer lies where the two come together.*

Before logging off, Leilani printed out their dialogue in hopes it would have more meaning for her later. There seemed to be nothing left to do but follow Rainy's advice. She gathered her dream journal, the notes from her first two regression sessions, the tape from her Wyoming trip and a fresh pad to write on. Remembering how stressful the last session had been, she decided to get that out of the way first. She purposefully kept her eyes open the whole time and repeatedly reminded herself that none of it was actually happening to her.

Two hours later she felt like a dishrag again, despite her attempts to remain separated from Meg. On one hand, she hoped nothing ever happened to her in this lifetime that would cause so much heartache. On the other hand, she hoped that this life did not end before she had the opportunity to love and be loved as Meg had.

To shake off the sadness, Leilani made some lunch and watched the news, but it didn't ease her troubled heart. She knew the only thing that was going to make her smile today was to find the man and prevent the disaster.

She began her review by carefully studying the notes she'd made of the regression sessions. Again, she found the common elements, including the man's name. She reread Rainy's answer. Where did the two come together? What were the commonalities between the regressions and her dreams?

She slowly went over all her notes from each dream sequence, specifically looking for anything that correlated with the regression sessions. *Where did the two come together?* In Saint Domingue, there was a mass murder, as there was in her vision of Carnaval Miami. That was a clear connection that defined what was going to happen.

In Salem, Joseph had been trapped in a cell, looking out a window when Hannah was hung. This was somewhat similar to the dream she had of him in the small room, but he was looking out at wide open country, not a village. Thus, it had the similar circumstance of his being unable to escape or help her, but didn't help to pinpoint the location.

The only other possible similarity was that the third regression had taken her to the Wyoming Territory and the view out the man's window in her dream *could* have been in Wyoming. It wasn't much, but since it was all she had, she decided to do some research on Wyoming.

A great deal of the state was in the Rocky Mountain Range with lots of open, uninhabited areas and plenty of deep snow at this time of year. As to individual rock formations, Wyoming had plenty of those as well. Devil's Tower, in the northeast corner of the state, was proclaimed a national monument by Teddy Roosevelt, while Medicine Bow National Forest in the southeast corner was known for its many smaller rock formations in all sorts of shapes. It was also easy to confirm that Wyoming had buffalo. Yellowstone National Park in the northwestern corner had a great herd of the beasts, and a lot of sites in the northern part were named after the famous showman, *Buffalo* Bill. If that wasn't enough, the Wyoming state flag had a buffalo on it.

An hour later, she knew enough about Wyoming to make her want to visit one day but she was no closer to confirming where her man was. Giving up on the internet, she pulled out her atlas and turned to the detailed map of the state. For several seconds she just stared at it.

"Come on, Joseph. I'm trying to help but you've got to give me a clue. Turn a searchlight on or something." She let her gaze roam over the map, hoping that one location would draw her attention more than the rest, but no lights came on.

Phyllis had said the last regression had cemented their bond and she wanted that to be true, but she didn't know how to reach him with her conscious mind. Her gifts tended to go to sleep when she woke up—

Suddenly she realized that Phyllis had shown her how to pull back the veil and operate both parts of her mind at once. She knew what she had to try next.

She poised her right index finger above the map of Wyoming and closed her eyes. One breath at a time she guided herself into a state of deep meditation and focused on an image of Joseph in the room with the calendar and the boarded-up window, exactly as he appeared in her dreams.

Once she had the visual fixed, she took herself into that room. The expression on his face was a mixture of bewilderment and pleasure.

"Hello, Joseph. My name is Leilani. I'm trying to help you."

"Are you an angel?"

She laughed. *"Not even close."*

"You're real?"

"Yes. Please take my hand so I can find you."

He reached out and clasped her hand. *"Don't go to the Carnaval."*

"I won't," she promised and began to leave.

"Wait!"

She returned to him.

"I love you."

Leilani's eyes popped open and the connection was broken. Those three words were certainly not what she was expecting him to say. Further contemplation about that was halted when she realized her index finger was pressing on a spot on the map. Carefully she raised her hand and read the words her fingertip had covered. A strong, head-to-toe shiver confirmed that her dream man was in Carbon County, near the North Platte River, west of Cheyenne.

* * * * *

Joseph's head jerked upright and he quickly looked around to get his bearings. He and several others had been watching a movie when he dozed off. He was almost surprised that he was still there, with them, and that the same movie was still on. A glance at the clock confirmed that he hadn't been out for more than a few minutes.

And yet he would have sworn he was back in his own room and that *she* had come to visit him there. He had heard of guys going "stir-crazy" but never experienced it himself.

As subtly as possible he shifted in his chair to hide the effect his dream woman had on him.

He assumed the dream was triggered by his constant prayer for a miracle, but at least now his imagination had given her a name as beautiful as she was...*Leilani*.

* * * * *

Leilani quickly weighed her options. The logical step would be to call Neil and give him the county name to pass on to his FBI friend. The instant she formed the thought, her stomach soured and she realized that if the authorities acted on such a vague tip, the "mob" might get wind of their approach and have time to take off before they were caught. Her nightmares of death and destruction would not be prevented from happening and the present-day Joseph might be killed. No, she had to be able to give them something much more precise.

Although she had never before gotten physically involved in solving any of the problems or crimes she had dreamed about, this one was totally different. This time, because of the karma between her and Joseph, she was already physically involved. This time she was going to have to do more than just sleep on it.

Returning to the internet, she did a search on Carbon County and was very pleasantly surprised at the wealth of historical information she found. She was further elated when she found one site that listed the names of the pioneers who settled in the county prior to Wyoming becoming a state. But when she saw the name Robert O'Donnell, she felt as though she'd won the lottery.

O'Donnell was listed as a cattle rancher whose spread had been adjacent to the North Platte River. A few clicks later, she discovered that a resort/dude ranch called Dudes & Dolls Ranch was now on that property. Leilani's excitement peaked when she went to the resort's website and read its history.

About a hundred years ago, the O'Donnell Ranch was sold and slowly parceled off. However, the dude ranch's claim to fame was that it had restored the main house, bunkhouse and other buildings to their original condition.

Without a moment's hesitation, she called the number on the ranch's website and asked to speak to the owner, Ken Adler.

"This is Ken. What can I do for you?"

Leilani had no idea what she was going to say before it came out of her mouth. "Hello. My name is Leilani Wakefield. I'm doing research for an article on dude ranch vacations for a prominent travel magazine. I'm hoping to include Dudes & Dolls in the article."

"Why, that would be wonderful. I never turn down a chance to tell people about this place, but if this is just a solicitation for advertising, I'm afraid—"

"Oh no. I'm not selling anything, I swear. And quite honestly, your website does a good job of showing off the ranch for the average vacationer. The reason I'm calling is to confirm the fact that the buildings are still in original condition and not torn down and rebuilt as replicas. That's more the focus of my article."

"As a matter of fact, that happens to be something we're very proud of here. Actually, we were quite fortunate that the former owners took such good care of the place. We even have a considerable amount of the furniture and other artifacts that belonged to Robert O'Donnell. He had no heirs, you see, so when he passed away, everything was sold along with the ranch. I could email you some photographs that aren't on the website, if that would help."

"I was thinking more along the lines of taking the photos in person." Leilani couldn't believe she'd just said that.

"Oh, I see. Well, we're not operational right now. Too much snow for our brand of tourists."

"That doesn't matter. As I said, I'm more interested in the buildings than the outdoor activities, um…especially the interiors. Would it be possible for me to get a room for a day or two this week? Of course, I'll pay whatever the regular rate is."

Mr. Adler's delight was clear in his voice. "Absolutely. It will be such a pleasure to have a guest. When might I expect you?"

"Tomorrow, if I can get a flight out." Again Leilani wondered who said that. "Is there an airport closer than Cheyenne?"

"There's a small one in Rawlins, but at this time of year—"

"No small airport for me. I'll fly into Cheyenne and rent a car. Your site showed that it's about a two-hour drive, right?"

"Yes, as long as the roads are clear, which they are right now. No more snow has been predicted this week, but make sure you rent a four-wheel drive vehicle just in case."

"Will do. I'll call you back to confirm after I arrange my flight."

Chapter Fourteen

"Come here, princess."

She felt him tug gently on her apron strings. "But the dishes —"

"Can wait. I can't."

She turned and met his gaze...and instantly forgot about the after-dinner mess. There was no possible resistance to that look in his eyes. He was slowly closing in on her mouth when she had a moment of clarity. "Leila?"

"She was sound asleep before I finished the first verse of her lullaby." He moved to kiss her again but held his lips a breath away. "Anything else?"

She smiled and closed the distance between them. For several seconds she focused on making his knees as weak as hers.

With great effort, he broke the kiss and murmured into her ear. "If you had cleaned up the kitchen like a good wife should, I'd take you right here, but as it is..."

She nipped his earlobe. "I've already wiped off the table."

He raised his head and grinned. "Have I told you yet today how much I love you?"

Leilani woke up when she tried to snuggle deeper into her pillow and found it impossible to roll over. It took another moment to remember that she was on an airplane, with her seatbelt securely fastened and her knees pressed against the seatback in front of her.

She still felt a little tingly from the steamy dream. Was it a prediction of something wonderful to come or just an assurance that her decision to go to Wyoming would lead to his rescue? Or was it a scene from another lifetime she and Joseph had shared?

The apron seemed to suggest an earlier time, maybe the fifties. It all seemed to be meshed together now—the past, the present, the future, the dreams and the regressions. Whatever this dream represented, it felt nice to believe that, at some time, they were in love and had a baby girl.

She could still barely believe that she was on her way to Cheyenne, but as soon as she had voiced her intention to Mr. Adler, she knew she had to go. She had no idea what she would do once she got there but she had complete faith that the best course of action would come to her.

Luck and the weather were both on her side all day and she reached the Dudes & Dolls Ranch just as the sun was setting. She had seen photos of the buildings on the website, but as she pulled up to the main house she was assailed with a powerful sense of déjà vu that had nothing to do with the photos. She knew this place *personally* and the feelings associated with it were mostly bad. Even though she had no previous experience like this, she was certain it was going to take a lot of energy to keep the past separated from the present in this place.

On the positive side, however, there was something going on inside her body that was reminiscent of what she felt when she was dreaming of the man she now called Joseph. It was enough to convince her that she was very, very close to him now.

The front door opened before she could ring the bell. "You must be Leilani. I'm Ken Adler." She was a little surprised to see that he was decades older than he'd sounded over the phone. He took the overnight case from her and carried it inside. "Hope you don't mind that I'm not wearing my cowboy garb to greet you. I'll be happy to get dolled up for some pictures tomorrow if you'd like."

She smiled and started to tell him that wasn't necessary but at the last second, she remembered she was supposed to be a journalist. "I'd hate to put you out, but it would be nice to have a photo with the owner in it."

His expression let her know that was the appropriate answer. "I have a casserole in the oven for dinner, but it will wait a few more minutes if you'd like the quickie tour."

"That would be wonderful. Thank you."

Though wood had been varnished, walls repainted and various pieces of western-style décor added, Leilani recognized the rooms she had seen in her regression session. When she entered the bedroom where Meg had slept, she got a chill that caused her to visibly shake.

"This room is always colder than the rest of the house," Mr. Adler explained immediately. "In the summer that's a good thing, but at this time of year, there doesn't seem to be enough wood in Wyoming to warm up this room. This was Mrs. O'Donnell's quarters and the local legend is that her spirit is still here."

"Really?" Leilani replied in the curious tone she assumed would be expected. "I've heard of haunted houses, of course, but I've never stayed in one. I didn't notice that tidbit on your website."

Mr. Adler chuckled. "We don't mention it on the website or in the brochure because it could put some tourists off. Word of mouth seems to work best on that score."

"Well, it doesn't put me off at all. In fact, I'd love to hear the story."

"Actually, there are several versions, but for our visitors, I tend to stick with the story that begins with Meg Kearney, a poor Irish immigrant, barely surviving in New York City. To escape her circumstances, she answered Robert O'Donnell's ad for a bride and he sent for her. It is said that he fell in love with her at first sight but that her heart had already been given to a man she had left behind in Ireland. She did everything she could to repay him for saving her from a life of slaving in a workhouse, but what he wanted from her, she just couldn't give him. Finally, after a few years, she got pregnant and for the first time, she seemed to be making him happy. Unfortunately, his joy was short-lived. She miscarried and bled to death."

"*Oh!* How terrible." The tale he related had similarities to what she had seen in the regression, but there were a few major missing elements, like O'Donnell's cruelty, impotence, an Indian lover and a double homicide. She had to bite her lip not to tell him what really happened.

"Yes, definitely not a happily-ever-after fairy tale. He never remarried either. Thus, no heirs. Some people say she is still hovering around trying to make people happy since she failed O'Donnell."

"Oh. Well, at least that's a ghost story that shouldn't scare anyone away." Leilani knew for a fact that Meg wasn't hanging around because ghosts are disembodied spirits that haven't gone into the light and thus, can't be reincarnated. And she had no doubt about being the reincarnation of Meg. Rather than the presence of a disembodied spirit, she sensed old, negative energy and, in this case, it was enough to keep the room chilly year-round.

Or there could just be a draft that no one bothered to fix in order to keep the ghost story alive.

"I have to admit, you've got me intrigued. Would you mind if I stayed in this room?"

"Not at all. I'll bring you some extra blankets and the space heater. But I have to be honest…despite the stories, no one has ever claimed to have seen our ghost. Maybe you'll get lucky and she'll appear to you. Then you'd really have something different to write in your article!"

Mr. Adler continued to relate other stories as he showed her the rest of the house. Some were even true. "Tomorrow, I'll show you the bunkhouse, barn and stables. Of course, the guest bungalows are newer construction, but I'm sure you'll want to see those as well. It's supposed to be a clear, sunny day, so you should have lots of light for photographs."

"That would be perfect." She made a mental note to actually take some pictures. "I was also wondering if you might have a map of the area. I'd like to drive around a bit."

"Of course. Just remind me in the morning and I'll dig one up. Now how about some of my famous beef and macaroni casserole?"

As soon as she could politely excuse herself after dinner, she retired to Meg's room and headed straight for the dressing area where she had *seen* Meg hide her diary. Careful not to damage anything she could not repair later, she pried off a piece of baseboard and found the hidden niche behind it. With her head on the floor, she peered inside and gasped.

There, covered with dust and cobwebs, was a leather-bound book.

Her heart raced with anticipation as she gently removed the diary and blew off some of the dust. With the greatest care, she opened the cover and read the handwritten words on the first yellowed page.

This diary is the private property of Margaret Kearney, begun on the 30th day of April, 1870.

Once certain that the pages would not disintegrate with her touch, Leilani started reading Meg's own story. Despite the childish scrawl and misspelled words, she felt herself being taken back to when she was Meg, sailing across the Atlantic Ocean with great hope in her heart. There were sporadic notes written during her years in New York, some sad, as when her mother died, and some disappointing, as the years went by with little relief.

Meg's hope was fully restored when she read O'Donnell's ad. Then the entries became less frequent again as the reality of her new life in Wyoming set in, until she stopped writing completely for nearly two years. When Joseph Blackhawk arrived, she got back to her habit of making nightly entries, as her despair changed to optimism once again.

Leilani was jolted back to the present as she read the passage about the first time Meg and Joseph made love. Feeling that there was something very important about it, she slowly reread the words and concluded that the watering hole's location was the clue she'd been looking for. She had an incredibly strong feeling that where Meg's sanctuary had once been, Joseph could be today. From what Meg had written, it sounded as though it was a considerable distance northeast of the main house. Now all she had to do was find out exactly where that spot was.

She almost raced from the room to ask Mr. Adler for the information then remembered he had already promised to find her a map in the morning. It would make more sense to ask questions about the area while she was looking at a map.

Rather than return the diary to its hiding place, she packed it in her bag. After she got back home, she intended to mail it to the local historical society and let them decide whether the folk tale about Robert O'Donnell should be corrected.

Before going to bed, she remembered that her cell phone needed to be charged and saw that she had a voice message. Unfortunately, she had no signal to enable her to listen to it. There was no choice but to wait until she was driving around tomorrow.

* * * * *

Joseph lay on his cot, staring at the ceiling. He was no longer assuming that his dreams meant that someone was looking for him. Instead, the strange dreams he'd been having pretty much convinced him that he was losing his mind. But what a nice way to go. Rather than fretting over how Earl Junior was going to kill him, he was constantly daydreaming about his beautiful Polynesian princess. *Leilani.*

He didn't know what had spooked Earl, but the timetable for departure had suddenly been moved up. The plan originally called for the trucks to pull out on March 7 and drive straight to

Miami. Now they were heading out on the second—just two days away—and the route was being kept secret.

It occurred to him that Leilani—if, in fact, there was such a person and if she was actually a fellow agent—could be getting closer to figuring out where he was. Since Skip had found out that the Bureau had assigned an investigator to them a year ago, he might also have just learned that they were on their way to break up the party before it got started. Regardless, if the guys in the white hats didn't ride in within forty-eight hours, it would be too late for him.

Earl Junior had been given permission to use him for target practice before they headed out.

* * * * *

Considering her physical location and the strong possibility that Joseph was nearby, Leilani had closed her eyes fully expecting to have an entire night of exhaustive dreaming. On the contrary, she woke up feeling anxious but without any recollection of having dreamed a thing. Normally when the dreams ended, it meant the current problem or question had been resolved and her subconscious was taking a break. Since nothing about this series of dreams had been normal, however, she could not trust that everything was fine. In fact, the acid in her stomach suggested that it was quite the opposite of fine.

She had to force herself not to rush through the big breakfast Mr. Adler had prepared for her. The elderly man was obviously tickled to have a live person to talk to, and talk he did. She heard all about his wife's fatal heart attack five years ago and how lonely he was afterward. Thankfully, his son had turned him onto surfing the internet to fill the time when the ranch wasn't overflowing with guests. It sounded like he spent most of his days in various chat rooms with his internet acquaintances.

When a phone call interrupted his monologue, she took advantage of the break to fetch her camera and started taking pictures inside the house for her fictitious article. For the next hour, he escorted her around the property so that she could photograph the other buildings as well. It was late morning before she was able to ask him for the map of the area he had mentioned.

He found a detailed map of Carbon County and spread it out on the kitchen table. To help orient her, he pointed out the ranch's location, the road she'd come in on and how to get to the county seat of Rawlins. "A lady friend of mine works at the town hall there and I'm sure she'd be glad to give you some flyers about local historical sites you might be interested in."

"I heard there are a lot of unusual rock formations in the area. Could you point some of those out? They usually make good photo ops." She got a pen out of her bag and prepared to mark any spots he pointed to.

"Actually, there are quite a few, but only the really big ones are going to be visible above the snow. You might try these." He pointed to three spots, one of which was in a northeasterly direction.

Near that spot, she saw a small area of blue. "What's this here?"

He adjusted his glasses on his nose. "Just a pond. Covered with snow now, of course."

Her heart was racing. She felt certain that was the watering hole she was looking for. "So how much of this was the original O'Donnell Ranch?"

With his index finger, he marked the old boundary.

"Wow, it sure was huge." Trying to keep her voice sounding casual, she asked, "How much do you own?"

"This parcel here," he said with a proud grin, as he again used his finger to mark the borders.

"And what about this property up here?" Her hand shook slightly as she pointed her pen at the pond.

He frowned then shook his head. "I'm really not sure. Heard that some sort of computer company bought the land and put a few buildings on it so they could use it as a training facility. But no one's there now."

Leilani felt a fluttering in her stomach but wasn't sure if it was because she was on the right track or if Mr. Adler had just said something important. She quickly folded up the map, thanked him and headed out the door.

With the map on the front seat next to her, Leilani started going east in the direction she had come in from until she came to a road that would take her north. Since there was virtually no one else on the road, she was able to drive very slowly. She let her gaze roam over every foot of the vast countryside, in hopes that something would light up for her. Snow had been cleared from the main roadways, but otherwise the land was covered in a white blanket. She could see an occasional house or barn, as well as fences and trees rising above the snow. There was no way to accurately read mileage on the map Mr. Adler had given her, so she was counting on her body to let her know when she was getting close.

She had barely been driving a half hour when she saw it—the rock shaped like a double smokestack. Leilani hadn't thought to bring binoculars, but there was a way to get a better view of the area than from behind the wheel of the car. Hoping no one else would drive by, she got out of the car and climbed up on the roof. In the distance, she could make out the rooftops of a cluster of buildings, but there was no plowed roadway between them and where she was. According to the map, there was no other road that would take her any closer than this one either. She climbed down from her perch and got back in the car.

Closing her eyes, she took several slow, deep breaths and pictured Joseph in her mind.

Joseph. Are you there in those buildings? Am I close?

* * * * *

Joseph froze in his tracks, whipping his head from left to right. *Leilani?* It was one thing to dream about her, but he was wide awake now and would swear she had just called his name. Talk about wishful thinking! *Hang in there, honey, dreamtime is only about ten hours away and I promise to give you my undivided attention then.*

* * * * *

Leilani's eyes opened wide as she felt the wave of sexual need flood through her. *What the heck was that?* It took her only a second to correlate it with the feelings aroused in her by Joseph Browning, Joseph Blackhawk and the husband in the dream she'd had on the plane. She needed no further confirmation. He was there, in one of those buildings. After making sure the mark she'd placed on the map earlier seemed to match up with where she was now, she checked her cell phone for a signal. Her carrier obviously had no tower this far out. She figured her best bet was to head for Rawlins.

By the time she reached the Rawlins town limits, she had a signal and was finally able to listen to her voice messages.

"Leilani, this is Gayle, a friend of Neil's. The information you gave him sounds exactly like something we've been looking for. Please call me back as soon as possible. My number should be on your caller ID, but it would be best if you called me from a land line."

This was followed by two messages from Neil. The first was a checkup call. The second was frantic and scolding at the same time.

"I just talked to Tillie. Have you lost your mind? What could you be thinking? Okay. Just call me as soon as you get this. And you really need to call Gayle too. If I wasn't so worried, I'd be furious. Okay. Call me."

Finally, there was an apology from Tillie, mimicking the voice of an old gangster movie star.

"Sorry, I squealed to the copper, baby. But I had no choice. He hung me out the window and threatened to drop me on my head."

Leilani decided she had one more thing to do before returning the calls. She parked behind the Rawlins Town Hall and went in to do a little research and reconnaissance. One of the best things about small towns was that there was always someone with enough time to talk to strangers. In no time at all, Leilani found her information source, who just happened to be the lady friend Mr. Adler had mentioned. Leilani remembered to ask for some of the flyers he'd suggested then worked the conversation around to the O'Donnell Ranch.

The very accommodating lady told her some of the same facts she already knew and a few tidbits she didn't. Soon enough Leilani found an opening to ask what she really wanted to know.

"Why yes, I'm familiar with that parcel," the lady said. "It was bought by a corporation a few years ago."

Leilani gave up trying to get information subtly. "Would you know the name of the corporation? I'd be interested in contacting them."

"Certainly. It's a matter of public record in the tax collector's office. Give me a second to pull it up for you." She used her computer for a few minutes. "Well, now this is interesting. The corporation's address is shown as being in the Bahamas and it looks like it bought another large, adjacent parcel a few months ago." She printed out a copy of what she'd found and gave it to Leilani. "The corporate name and address are there. Can I help you with anything else?"

"No, that's it. Thank you so much for your help." Leilani took the page and had to stop herself from running out the door. At the last instant she remembered to ask, "Oh, could you direct me to a pay phone?"

Twenty minutes later, she had made her call to Gayle, passed on everything she had and was able to enjoy lunch in a small cafe. The FBI Special Agent said very little in response to either the psychic or researched information. Leilani received such a wonderful shiver of confirmation and sense of relief when she hung up that she felt certain she had accomplished her mission. The lingering dream images of impending doom were dissipating. She chose to believe that meant Joseph's life was no longer in danger.

On the way out of town, a statue of a cowboy caught her eye and she thought to add it to the collection of pictures she'd taken thus far. That was when she realized that, in her haste to go exploring, she had made a tactical error. *She didn't have her camera.* She had left it on the table at the ranch. A real journalist...or a real undercover investigator...would probably have noticed that immediately and turned around to retrieve it. But she was neither, and now that she had completed her mission, she figured it really didn't matter.

Before she left Rawlins, she used her cell phone to call Tillie and assure her that she didn't mind her squealing to the copper. The final call was to Neil.

"It's about time you called!" he barked in place of a greeting. "I've been worried sick. What the hell could you be thinking, taking off like that! Do you have any idea how much danger you might have put yourself in? At least I could have gone with you if you had told me!"

"So, basically, you're just mad that I didn't include you in the fun!" She gave him a chance to calm down a bit. "Listen, I'm fine and definitely not doing anything heroic by myself. I just hung up from talking to Gayle. I think everything is going to be okay now."

"You *think*? You mean you can't tell?"

"I mean, I'm pretty sure. At least I don't feel compelled to be here anymore."

"Good. Then get your butt back home where it belongs!"

She chuckled. "I have a flight back tomorrow morning."

He exhaled heavily. "Okay. I gotta tell you, pal, Gayle couldn't explain what's going on, but it was pretty obvious that you were on to something major. I'm just glad you're safe and coming home."

Mr. Adler looked unusually relieved upon her return to the ranch. "After you left, I got to thinking that I should have gone with you. I mean, what sort of host was I to send you off with nothing more than a map? But here you are, safe and sound again. How about some coffee and devil's food cake? I made it this morning."

Leilani could tell he was distressed, but she'd only been gone a few hours, hardly long enough to cause him to worry about her. Maybe he was just worried that she'd gone back home before he had a chance to tell her more of his stories. "Coffee and cake sound good."

His instant relief convinced her that she had guessed right. He simply wanted the company. A few minutes later he had her afternoon pick-me-up on the kitchen table, with a cup of tea and some dietetic cookies for himself.

As soon as she sat down, he launched into the story of how he ended up in Wyoming. A very long time ago, he and his late wife had honeymooned at a dude ranch and decided they would run one themselves after he retired.

Leilani didn't mind listening to him talk. She was completely relaxed now that she had done what she'd come here to do. The coffee hit the spot but the cake had an aftertaste that she didn't care for. However, she finished it rather than insult him.

"It was in the sixties that it all started, you know. Immigration laws were passed for a reason, and yet when those boats started arriving in Miami, the politicians welcomed them with open arms."

What was he talking about? Leilani realized she had let her mind wander as he chattered about one thing or another. Fortunately, he didn't need her comments or agreement to continue.

"So, boo-hoo, Castro turned out to be a big bad communist! Well, the damned Cubans put him in power. Why was it our responsibility to offer citizenship to any of them who could make it across ninety miles of water? And if that wasn't bad enough, in the eighties, Castro decided to clean up his shit-hole island by sending all their criminals and diseased to Miami. And what did our politicians do?"

Leilani blinked at him, trying to focus her vision that had strangely become very blurry. He no longer seemed to be a sweet, lonely old man. He sounded more like a fanatical bigot.

He didn't need her answer to go on. "They welcomed the lower life forms right into this country. Did you know they even created a policy called wet-foot, dry-foot? All some damn Cuban has to do is set one foot on our land and they get to stay. Hell, you'd think after 9/11, they'd get the message and close the doors, but no, they just keep welcoming the bastards in, letting them take jobs away from Americans.

"Yep. There's no doubt about it. This whole business of letting foreigners hold our country hostage started in Miami. You know, my wife and I visited Miami once, on vacation. Everywhere we went people spoke Spanish, like it wasn't even part of the United States."

"Miami?" Leilani repeated, but she heard her own voice from a distance. He was saying words that made alarms go off in her head. *Miami. Cubans.* Words that were connected to the terrible thing she wanted to prevent. *"Why…are you…telling me about…this?"* She was so drowsy she could barely force the words out.

"Just thought you might want to know why we chose Miami for our statement."

"We? You're…involved?"

He looked surprised. "You sound as though you didn't know that. Why would the FBI send you here if they didn't know— Oh, I see. The Feds found out about Miami and the house in Wyoming, but not about me." He chuckled over that. "Well, how about that. You ended up in my home by accident!"

He thought she was an FBI agent? She tried to object but couldn't form the words.

"Let me save you the trouble Miss Wakefield, or whatever your name really is. You are not a journalist. I couldn't help but wonder why you were so insistent about coming here at such an unseasonable time. And you had to have paid an exorbitant rate for a next-day airline ticket. Not exactly a rational expense for a little article. Then, not only do you *not* have a professional camera, you missed taking photos of some of the best things. What cinched it for me though was when you forgot to take the camera with you today."

The damn camera. What was it she had thought about the camera? She tried to find the answer, but she couldn't remember why it was important.

"So I asked myself, what sort of travel writer would drive off without her camera? Then I called the magazine you said you work for. They never heard of you. On the other hand, a little birdie warned us that an FBI agent was asking some questions about Carnaval Miami and Wyoming, and then you show up here the next day. And today you were much too interested in a particular piece of property that we've taken great pains to keep secret.

"By the way, that was very foolish of you to ask questions of my friend in Rawlins. She called me right after you left to let me know how helpful she had been. She thought she was doing me a favor. In a way, she was." Again, he found humor in the situation.

Leilani's eyelids drooped closed and no matter how hard she tried, she could not raise them again. One more thing got through the mud building up in her brain before everything went dark.

She had been drugged.

Chapter Fifteen

"We got a surprise for you, Vic."

Joseph looked up from the weight bench he was lying on to see Butch, Ned and Earl Junior closing in on him. They were all smiling, as though he was about to be the target of a practical joke. He reset the weights he was pressing and sat up. With a fixed grin on his face, he mentally prepared to defend himself. "Yeah? Well, I'm only about halfway through my workout so unless it's a broad, it'll have to wait."

All three howled as though he had said something really hilarious. "Just come with us," Earl Junior coaxed. "The surprise is in your room."

The hair on the back of Joseph's neck was practically vibrating, warning him of danger. He quickly weighed his options. He could refuse, take them on right here and possibly get killed in the process. Or he could play along and get killed later. There was no question in his mind that his number was up one way or the other. It was just a matter of when.

He had seen the last-minute activity going on all day. As soon as it got dark, a driveway from the garage to the main road had been plowed. The trucks would definitely be pulling out at sunrise.

The three men stayed close behind Joseph on the way to his room. When he hesitated to open the door, Butch did it for him then nudged him inside.

Thoughts of retaliating were erased the instant he saw the sleeping woman on his cot. "Lei—"

He cut off her name but not before the shock of seeing his dream woman was revealed in his expression.

"Tie them up," Skip ordered as he rose from a chair in the corner of the room.

Joseph didn't stand a chance of escape. A few minutes later, he and Leilani, who he now realized was unconscious, were strapped to wooden chairs and tied together, back-to-back. He wondered what they had given her and hoped she'd awaken soon. Any chance they might get to escape would be a lot harder if he had to carry her out. He laughed to himself as he realized how extremely optimistic that thought was.

Skip instructed Ned and Earl Junior to get back to work while he questioned the prisoners. Butch was to remain and guard the door. Before leaving, Earl Junior demanded a promise that he would be called back in for the big finish.

"You want to tell me what this is all about?" Joseph demanded, with considerably more bravado than he felt.

"Sure," Skip said agreeably. "Right after you tell me who she is."

"I have no idea."

Skip nodded and motioned for Butch to give him a hand, literally.

Miraculously, Joseph's jaw did not crack from the blow Butch dealt him.

"That was stupid. Why waste getting your pretty face messed up over the easy questions? You obviously recognized her and you even started to say the name on her driver's license."

Joseph shook his head. "I'm not lying. I don't know her. But she looked familiar. Maybe I met her somewhere."

Skip smirked at him. "Somewhere? How about recognized her because you're both FBI agents?"

"Agents?" Joseph managed to sound completely incredulous. "I don't know about her, but I've been living with you for a year now. You probably know me better than my own mother. I've been part of everything this group has done, one hundred percent committed. Hell, *you* can't even say that!"

Butch stepped forward to assist again, but Skip held up a hand to stay him. "I'll grant you that much. You've never given us a reason to question your loyalty. But we know we were infiltrated by the FBI at the time you joined up. Then, the other day, we learned that a female agent was asking questions about our little project. This one shows up here right afterward and basically gives herself away."

Skip walked around the chairs and tipped Leilani's head back so that it bumped Joseph's. "Beautiful woman, but not much of a spy. At any rate, deny all you want, but I was looking at your face when you walked in. I am absolutely positive that you know her. And we know she's an agent. It's not much of a leap to deduce that you're an agent as well. Personally, I've always had my suspicions about you. You're just way too intelligent to be a follower."

"Okay," Joseph said. "Just for argument's sake, let's say you're right. Why are we both still alive?"

Skip chuckled. "For one thing, your present circumstances are very temporary. But on the remote chance that we might need a hostage or two, Earl has decided to keep you both alive...for the moment."

"I don't follow, why would you need hostages?"

"I know you haven't gotten word out. So we weren't expecting any surprise visits from your friends. Unfortunately, the pretty lady was out and about today without an escort. So we have no way of knowing if she figured out anything important or whether she passed word on to anyone else." He snorted. "But based on her slip-ups, I'm betting we're still completely in the clear. I'll know for sure once I question her."

Joseph heard an opening to get one of the answers he needed. "That would have been easier if you hadn't knocked her out. What'd you give her anyway?"

Skip made a face. "Just a couple of crushed-up sleeping pills, but she's been out for about six hours already. I figured she'd be awake by now."

"Are you sure she's alive?" Skip didn't reply, but Joseph knew the answer to that because he felt her heart beating along with his. "Why don't you use an ammonia inhalant? There are some in the first-aid kits."

Skip looked at him skeptically but then sent Butch off to fetch a kit. "Not quite sure why you're being so helpful."

"Hey, the sooner you question her, the faster you'll realize this is all a mistake."

"There have been some mistakes made, but this isn't one of them."

Joseph heard a note of disapproval and pounced on it while Butch was still absent. "Can I ask you a personal question?"

"You can always ask."

"What are you doing here?"

That brought a grin to Skip's face. "I don't suppose you're trying to start a philosophical discussion."

"We can save that for the road trip to Miami," Joseph returned in the same lighthearted tone. "I'm serious. Regardless of what your personal opinions are, you don't really fit in with the others. Frankly, I don't think you're passionate enough to actually *hate* any entire group of people."

Skip's grin spread into a full smile. "I'm not sure if I've just been insulted or complimented. You're such a smart guy. Why do *you* think I'm here?"

"Earl walks around here acting like he's the head honcho. But you're really the one with the power, aren't you?" Skip simply arched a brow. "You're in control of all the communications and, as far as I can tell, the money. Whoever controls those two things is the real power. Am I getting warm?" Until the words were out of his mouth, Joseph had not fully realized that Skip was the unidentified brain of the beast.

Butch's return stopped Skip from responding. He wasted no time extracting the inhalant and waving it under Leilani's nose.

Leilani struggled to escape the acrid smell that had suddenly filled her sinuses. A moment later, she realized she was straining against actual physical bonds. It took several more seconds before she was conscious enough to question her surroundings.

Her vision slowly focused on a wall a few feet away from her. It was a wall with a boarded-up window...a wall she recognized immediately. More of the pungent odor wafted by and her head cleared a bit more. She registered the fact that she was sitting in the room she had seen in her dreams and that, for some reason, she was securely tied. Her automatic reaction was to try to wriggle out of the restraints.

"Don't waste your energy," a man murmured close to her ear. "The ropes will just scrape your skin."

I know that voice. "Joseph?"

Farther behind her, another male voice let out a sharp laugh. She swiveled her head from side to side but couldn't turn far enough to see anyone. She could, however, see broad male shoulders, covered in plaid flannel, very close to hers. It was also clear that she and the man, who she assumed was Joseph, were tied together.

"Try to relax," Joseph quietly commanded.

"Butch, get some tape for this one's mouth. In the meantime, another word from you...*Joseph,* and I'll make sure she suffers for it."

Who is speaking? For that matter, who is Butch? How did I get here? How did I end up tied to Joseph? She had a long list of questions but she hesitated to ask anything that would result in punishment.

A slightly built, middle-aged man stepped into her view. "Mr. Adler?" she asked without thinking.

"As a matter of fact yes, I am, only the first name's Skip," he said. "Was that a good guess or do I really look that much like my old man?"

"Oh! You're his son. He told me about how you taught him to use the computer to entertain himself. Did he drug me or did you?"

"No, that was his doing. Once we figured out who you were, he thought of a way to put you out of commission until it was decided what to do with you. He really can be a resourceful old guy when he needs to be."

Leilani's common sense told her to play dumb until she knew what they knew. "But I don't understand. Why would he want to drug me? Why am I here?"

"I'll make you the same offer I made Vic—or rather, Joseph. I'll tell you what this is all about right after you tell me how much the Feds know."

She angled her head up at him and narrowed her eyes in confusion. "The Feds? You mean, like, the government?" She congratulated herself on sounding truly bewildered. An instant later, Skip rewarded her with a hard slap across her face.

"*Hey!*" Joseph shouted.

Skip backhanded Leilani's other cheek. "I already warned you not to speak. Utter one more word and I'll turn her over to Butch. I heard he has some experience roughing up pretty ladies. Now where were we? Oh yes. You were pretending that you're not with the FBI."

"But I'm *not*," she protested.

He raised his hand again then lowered it. "All right. Who *do* you work for? And keep in mind that I already know you're not a travel writer."

Leilani's cheeks were stinging but no one ever died from excessive slapping. On the other hand, it sounded like Butch was someone she'd rather avoid. Unable to think of any lie he might believe, she opted for the truth.

"I promise to be completely honest but I warn you, it might sound a little…crazy."

Butch finally returned with a roll of electrical tape and swiftly used a piece to cover Joseph's mouth.

"Good," Skip said and sat down on the cot. "I've got this under control for the moment, Butch. Why don't you make the rounds and see if anyone needs help. I'll find you when I need you to relieve me for the night."

The thought of Butch being their sole guard for the night gave Leilani a sick feeling. If only she knew for sure that the information she gave Gayle was already being acted upon, she might be able to calm down. She had felt completely certain that her mission had been accomplished after she'd spoken to the FBI agent. She had assumed that meant the massive attack planned for Miami would be prevented.

What if her sense of relief had just meant there was nothing more she could do?

She had not wanted to believe that Joseph's life was still in jeopardy, yet it clearly was.

It had *never* occurred to her that her own life would be at risk. But the tragic endings of the three past lives she had seen should have been sufficient warning of how this would all end.

Skip stayed silent until Butch's footsteps faded, then said, "Okay, amuse me."

She heard Joseph inhale deeply and had the feeling he was trying to warn her to be careful. For the first time since she had awakened, she wondered if there was a chance that he felt any sort of connection to her.

"Well?" Skip prodded.

She licked her lips and tried to swallow. "I could really use a drink of water. Whatever I was given really dried my mouth out."

"I'll tell you what. I'll get you a drink if I like your story."

Leilani coughed, cleared her throat and quit stalling. "I'm not FBI, or any other kind of law enforcement officer. I own a little store in Melbourne, Florida. I have dreams about things before they happen. Sometimes I pass tips along to the police department."

Joseph cleared his throat at the same time Skip laughed out loud.

"Are you trying to tell me you're one of those psychic detectives, like on TV?"

"Not exactly," she said. "I don't have any abilities when I'm awake."

That solicited more laughter from Skip. "That's pretty obvious, since you never suspected my father's involvement. So tell me about your dreams."

Leilani gave him enough details about her dreams to have him wondering if she might be on the level. The oddest part about his reaction, however, was that he couldn't seem to stop laughing.

"And what did you tell the FBI?" he asked, obviously expecting to be further amused.

"I don't have a contact with the FBI. I only passed the warnings on to the Melbourne police. But I figured they hadn't done anything about it because I kept having the bad dreams. That's when I flew out here myself."

"To find this man you'd never met before?"

It was clear that Skip thought everything she was saying was hilarious, but she couldn't help but wonder what Joseph thought about it all. "To find him, and you, or rather your group. I simply *had* to find out something more specific to tell the police." She prayed that he could not see through the lies that she had woven in amongst the truth.

Skip scratched his head. "Well, you were right. That sounds crazy. But maybe just crazy enough to be true. Even Dad said he couldn't believe you were an agent. So let me see if I've got this right. You told some cops in Florida that you dreamed about a terrorist attack that would take place at Carnaval Miami on March 10, and that the people responsible might hate Cubans and were probably in Wyoming."

She nodded.

He cracked up again. "And what about the information you got in Rawlins?"

"You mean that a foreign corporation owns this property?"

"Exactly. Who have you told about that?"

She gave him her most confused look. "No one yet. I was just going to give it to the police and let them figure it out. I have a flight back tomorrow morning," she added, as though she really believed he would release her before then.

Skip smirked at her. "Don't count on making that flight." He rose from the cot and stepped out of her view.

"Wait!" she exclaimed to stop him. She wanted to delay being turned over to Butch as long as possible. "You promised me an explanation in return."

"So I did. But I lied."

"That's not fair. What does it matter anyway? I think it's obvious that you're not going to let me live to pass on anything I've learned, so why not just appease my curiosity?"

"You've got to be kidding, lady. What about this situation makes you think I'd play fair with you?"

Leilani scrambled for another straw to cling to. "But...um...at least tell me why you were laughing so much. Do you think I was making all that up? Do you still think I'm an FBI agent, after everything I've told you?"

"Hell no! I believe everything you said. The outrageous part is that the joke is on me!" After a moment's consideration, Skip shrugged. "You know what? I wouldn't really mind telling you the story from my point of view. At least it beats spending the next hour with the hillbilly outcasts. Not sure I can make mine as colorful as yours, but I think it'll hold your attention." He raised his voice a notch and added, "That goes for you too, Joe."

Joseph emitted a muffled grunt that suggested he wasn't expecting to hear anything worthwhile.

To Leilani's surprise, Skip crossed the room and closed the door before starting the promised explanation. Coming back into her view, he began with something she already knew.

"A few years ago, I turned my father onto surfing the net just to give him something to do. It didn't take him much time to find chat rooms with other men who shared his, shall we say, narrow views on politics. When he asked me to set up a website for him, I was just happy he'd found a new hobby and had stopped grieving over losing my mother. It never occurred to me that his hobby could be turned into a massive money machine."

"Money machine?"

"Oh yeah. You'd be surprised how many wealthy people will turn their assets over to fanatics, as long as the marketing material is slanted toward their personal prejudices."

Leilani was now genuinely curious. "I don't understand. What were you marketing?"

He grinned. "Secession from the United States government."

"What?"

"It's not quite as interesting as dreaming the future, but I figured that would get your attention. The website I originally set up was basically a forum for his new buddies to whine about the good ol' days and how America was being destroyed by all the politicians. Their favorite topic to bitch about was the government's lenient immigration policies."

Despite her drugged state at the time, Leilani recalled Mr. Adler ranting about that. "I gather none of them remembered that their own ancestors were once immigrants."

"Don't try to fit logic into any of this. It'll just give you a headache."

"Fine, but I'm still not seeing how you turned their bigotry into your profit."

Skip gave her another one of his sly grins. "All I did was offer them something they couldn't resist—a chance to start over, with a whole new country where *they* could decide who was allowed in. Once I started posting articles about forming a new America, open only to those they considered true Americans, the money started pouring in. I only had to use a little of it to buy some land and build this place."

"I'm sorry. Are you saying there are really people out there who believe it's possible to buy up a chunk of land within the United States and then simply make it their own country?"

He laughed. "Like I said, there's no logic here. A little creative writing convinced them we had found a loophole."

Joseph failed to stifle a groan, but Skip let it pass.

"I figured I'd have the whole thing shut down before anyone realized they'd been taken. Unfortunately, while I was playing my game out, my father and his cronies had awakened a sleeping dragon. You've probably heard a story or two about someone creating a monster that takes on a life of its own. Well, that's pretty much what happened here. A whole separate branch came together, determined to make a violent statement along with their demands to secede from the United States."

"Miami," she concluded simply.

"Right. The real shocker for me though, was that once the plan was born, even more money started flooding in. I'm not even sure where some of it came from."

Leilani felt her stomach convulse. "You…you could be dealing with foreign terrorists!"

Skip cocked his head. "Could be. I never figured it would get this far. Hell, I was sure the FBI would have put a stop to the whole thing as soon as the word 'secession' showed up on the web. I wasn't counting on Earl and the others being sharp enough to stay one step ahead of them."

This time, Joseph made a series of sounds in response to that statement.

"Yeah," Skip replied, as though he understood. "I knew the information we got about you being an agent was accurate. I just kept the certainty my own little secret. I was sure you'd figure a way to escape and put a stop to this whole thing before it got this far. At one point, I even tried to convince Earl to release you with false information, but he wouldn't hear it. Then I learned another agent might be on the way, and what do I end up with? A dreamer!" He let out a dry laugh and shook his head. "I guess the Feds aren't as with it as I thought they were."

"You can still stop it," Leilani insisted. "Release us tonight and we'll make sure they get captured on the road."

Skip shook his head. "Sorry babe, no can do. You'd have to tell them about me and my dad's parts in all this and I'm not okay with that. When the trucks head out in the morning, the old man and I will be going in a different direction...one that will take us out of the country."

"I didn't get the impression your father would go along with that."

"Probably not—which is why I have no intention of telling him ahead of time."

"What about the money?"

"It's safe."

"Then why haven't you left already?"

He laughed again. "It's not that complicated. If we took off early, there's always a chance they'd come after us. No one's expecting us to travel in the trucks with them tomorrow, so we're covered there. Besides, I wanted to make sure you hadn't arranged any surprises before I made my exit. And now I think I've answered enough of your questions. I'm going to bed. But don't get any ideas. Butch will be sitting with you until we're ready to go."

He walked toward the door then returned with a piece of tape, saying, "Almost forgot about this."

A few seconds later, Leilani's mouth was sealed and Skip was gone. *So much for getting that drink of water.*

Panic crept in almost immediately. She had hoped she could speak to Joseph before Butch came back. She had also thought there might be a chance of talking Butch into releasing her if she made him some sort of deal. A shiver of disgust followed the realization of what she might have to offer him and she knew she couldn't manage that.

While she had kept Skip talking she was able to avoid thinking about her circumstances, but reality now closed in on her with a vengeance. She felt the acid increase in her stomach. This wasn't a dream. She was really being held captive by people who intended to kill her. Everything she had imagined and hoped to have in the future was never going to come about.

The horrible, deadly karma she and Joseph shared in the past was about to happen again.

Images of Cassie, Hannah and Meg flashed through her mind. Remembering how the bond between her and Joseph kept strengthening, she tried to send him a telepathic thought.

Joseph?

She got no response, not even a wave of sensation as she had before. She supposed it was because she couldn't calm down enough to do it properly.

Suddenly she felt something touch her fingers and realized he was responding after all. Both their hands were tied behind their backs, close enough for him to link one of his fingers with hers. That small contact was the most incredible thing she had ever felt. Immediately, the panic and the acid ebbed and her heart slowed its pace.

She gently squeezed his finger, hoping he would understand how much she appreciated the gesture. The two squeezes he gave her in return made her relax that much more.

He then hummed four syllables that sounded like he was asking her if she was okay.

She was able to make a few similar sounds just before Butch strode in and plopped down on the cot with a comic book. His presence effectively put an end to any audible communication. Their night guard was as big and scary-looking as she had imagined a "Butch" would be. But as long as Joseph was touching her, she found that she could keep the panic in check.

* * * * *

Silent black helicopters...swarming like wasps in the dark sky...ropes unfurling...figures in white jumpsuits rappelling to the ground...orders shouted...explosive crashing...smoke everywhere...frantic, half-dressed men diving for cover...gunfire...

Leilani could feel herself being shaken but it still took a tremendous effort to wake up from the dream. When she finally surfaced she realized the shaking was Joseph, banging his chair against hers. He was making urgent sounds as loudly as he could. An instant later, she was assailed with the awareness that her dream fragments were actually happening all around her. One glance assured her that Butch was no longer in the room. She made as loud a sound as she could to let Joseph know she was awake.

"I think I found Grayson!" a man shouted from behind her.

Leilani heard the distinct sound of tape being ripped off Joseph's face.

"Get her outta here!" Joseph demanded.

Leilani's eyes began to burn just as a man in a white jumpsuit and a gas mask slashed a knife through their bonds. A blanket was dropped over her head and she was abruptly lifted over the man's shoulder. She tried to protest leaving Joseph behind but her rescuer was already on the run.

I didn't even have a chance to see his face.

Chapter Sixteen

Leilani glanced at the television on her kitchen counter. The news station was once again showing film of the property in Wyoming. Apparently, the paper trail of ownership from the off-shore corporation listed in the public records was still leading to a dead end. She had been home a week already, but the shocking report of the barely avoided terrorist attack was still a top news story. From one day to the next, details were gradually released to the public.

The FBI acknowledged that they had received a tip about a massive, deadly assault being planned by a radical group of secessionists. Recovered notes of plans, travel arrangements, detailed maps, estimated "kill" counts and so on, all confirmed the validity of the tip. An enormous stash of weapons, including remote-controlled incendiary bombs, were confiscated in the raid.

The evidence suggested that the group had planned a violent demonstration to be carried out at the Carnaval Miami. It was intended to be a protest to the United States' continuous open-door immigrant policy, despite continued terrorist attacks and threats by foreigners within our borders.

Several of the group's members had quickly turned into state witnesses and spilled everything they knew to save themselves. Leilani had no doubt that Skip had been at the front of that line. Between those confessions, Leilani's confidential testimony and the data recovered from Skip's computer, the number of arrests was staggering. The charges ranged from tax evasion to suspicion of treason. Ken Adler was the focus of the brightest spotlight, as every piece of evidence seemed to point right to his website. Unfortunately it could be months, or even years, before the whole thing was sorted out.

Sadly, the radicals did not surrender quietly. Two agents and three terrorists were killed and one more was in critical condition. The names of the casualties were given, and none of them were Joseph Grayson, nor did any of the photos of the deceased look familiar to Leilani. Yet she couldn't shake the feeling that she had lost him.

She repeatedly ordered herself not to think about the possibility that Joseph might still be one of the casualties. She had been so bonded to him that she could not help but feel the complete absence of the connection. Based on their past life karma, that surely did not bode well.

More curious was that Neil had been unable to learn anything about Joseph from Gayle. Despite all evidence to the contrary, she insisted there was no record of a missing agent named Joseph Grayson. Neil assured Leilani that he could very well still be under deep cover, but that didn't make her feel better.

The only thing that gave her any sense of peace about the situation was an online dialogue she had with Rainy. Once again, her Lotus Circle sister had pulled several tarot cards while they were chatting. Rainy was positive that the karma between her and Joseph was now completely balanced out. Leilani decided to interpret that to mean he was alive and well…somewhere.

But oh, how she wanted to know that for certain, to speak to him…to see his face. He wasn't even coming to her in dreams anymore.

He may not have been killed in the raid, but she was truly grieving over the loss of him and the love that never even had a chance.

* * * * *

Over the next few months, Leilani's daily routine was so well reestablished she could almost pretend the whole Wyoming experience had never occurred. Under the circumstances, she had little choice but to let it all go and get back to her nearly perfect life.

One evening as she was fixing dinner, there was a knock at her door. Peering through the security viewer, she could see a tall man wearing dark sunglasses. He had a scraggly, brown beard and similar hair sticking out from beneath a straw cowboy hat. She had no intention of answering the door for the stranger...until he removed the shades and looked directly into the viewer.

She would have known those dark eyes anywhere. She quickly pulled open the door and threw her arms around him. "*Joseph!* I thought I'd never see you again!" Abruptly releasing him, she stepped back and inspected him from head to toe. "Actually, this is the first time I've seen you at all outside of my dreams, and you don't look anything like I thought you would."

He shrugged and gave her a crooked grin as he stroked his beard. "This is pretty much how I've looked for the last year. I thought it was how you would recognize me. After all, the first time I saw you in Wyoming, you looked exactly the way I imagined you."

Leilani was only slightly surprised at that. "You imagined me?" He nodded. "You had dreams also?"

His grin widened to a sexy smile. "Very good ones, I might add. There were times when dreaming about you was the only thing that kept me sane."

She felt a wave of heat ripple through her. "Oh my...um, I'm glad I could help. I heard there were casualties. I was really worried. Why couldn't I find out if you were okay?"

"I was still undercover. It was clear that there was a leak inside the Bureau and I was the best shot at finding out who it was."

"And did you?"

He nodded. "Yep. As of this morning, it's finally over. But that's why I couldn't come see you before this."

"So your assignment ended this morning and you're here this evening. You didn't even stop to shave. Wow, I'm—" Suddenly she realized they were still standing outside. "Good heavens, where are my manners! Come in, come in." She stepped inside and held the door for him.

He remained where he was and his expression grew serious. "I just came by to say thank you. When you were telling Skip about your dreams, I wasn't sure how much of it was made up as a cover. You see, I had been guessing you were an agent. I might have thought it was all baloney but I was having some pretty crazy dreams at the same time you were. In fact, I even thought I heard you call my name once when I was wide awake. Since then, I found out everything you told Skip was the truth and that *you* were the one who tipped off the Bureau."

She tilted her head, looked up and waited for him to meet her eyes. The bond between them was so strong she couldn't believe he was able to resist, but he did. She tried another tack. "In other words, I probably saved your life."

"Yes," he uttered, with a slight crack in his voice.

"In which case, you at least owe me five minutes of conversation over a cup of coffee." She held out her hand.

He looked at her hand as though it were a live grenade. Visibly swallowing, he placed his hand in hers. The way his eyes closed and his shoulders relaxed confirmed that he felt the same incredible tingling sensation she did as it traveled from palm to palm and up their arms.

Yet he still held his ground. "I'm not sure what this is between us, but I feel like I have to tell you—coffee and five minutes of conversation might be all I can give you. I mean, I've been thinking a lot about making a big change in my life, but it may not take. As tempting as it might be to take this thing for a test run, there's a very good chance that it would never work."

She gave his hand a tug and he stepped over the threshold.

"Our backgrounds are totally different," he said with a lack of conviction.

She drew him all the way into her living room and pushed the door closed behind him.

"We come from completely separate worlds." Despite that statement, his arms slid around her waist and eased her against him.

"Really?" As she wrapped her arms around his neck, glimpses of their past lives flashed through her mind.

Drawing his head closer to hers, she brushed her lips over his and repeated, "Totally different backgrounds? Completely separate worlds? Believe me, Joseph—that never stopped us before."

The End

Enjoy an excerpt from:
Tarot of The Lotus Circle

Are you…

Living from one crisis to another?

Seeking information about business or finances?

Blocked by obstacles on every path?

Looking for love and finding only heartbreak?

Even if you have never seen a deck of Tarot cards before, *Tarot of The Lotus Circle* is so easy to learn, you'll be receiving answers to your questions and making predictions in no time at all.

The Universe is filled with things we cannot see with our physical eyes, but there are tools available to help us make good decisions, warn us of danger and inspire us to create new things. This book will help you take a giant step to a more enlightened human experience, beginning with an introduction to your personal Tarot Spirit Guide.

The Lotus Circle deck, layouts and interpretations are the result of a decade of messages and visions channeled by renowned medium Marilyn Campbell from her Spirit Guides. They directed her to share her knowledge of Tarot, insisting the material be simple enough for novices to get answers to their most perplexing questions. Under Their guidance, Marilyn modernized the images and interpretations while maintaining respect for the basic meanings and symbolism of the individual cards.

Tarot of The Lotus Circle walks you through the process of listening to your Guides, enhancing your intuition and reading the cards to solve problems and "see" into the future.

INTRODUCTION

Have you noticed how ancient practices have come back into public acceptance in recent years? In the field of medicine, we are seeing traditional physicians prescribing the use of herbs, acupuncture, magnets and so on as alternatives to chemicals and surgery. In science, quantum physicists have uncovered proof that our thoughts have the ability to affect our physical being. Psychiatrists have published articles and books giving evidence that reincarnation is a viable possibility and that someone suffering from multiple personality disorder could actually have one or more disembodied spirits manipulating his or her behavior.

In spiritual matters, many people are turning to ancient ideologies and religions for explanations about their existence. Those who once ridiculed others who believed in the occult are themselves now seeking the advice of metaphysical practitioners to predict upcoming events. Although I have been using my psychic gifts to assist clients for many years, I have never received as many inquiries as I do now.

With regard to my reading Tarot cards for myself and others, I am most frequently asked two questions:

Are Tarot cards evil?

The cards themselves have no powers. They are neither positive nor negative, good nor bad, light nor dark. I can assure you that if you set a deck on a table and walk away, they will do absolutely nothing on their own. They are simply metaphysical (spiritual or expanded consciousness) tools. How helpful they are depends completely on the reader and his or her ability to communicate with the spirit world, or The Other Side, as I refer to the dimension of love and light that exists on a different plane than Earth. When a reader bonds with a clean deck and has a strong connection with her Spirit Guides—beings of light who dwell on The Other Side but choose to assist those of us on the

Earthly plane—the hands of the reader (counselor) and/or the querent (person asking for information) will be spiritually guided as they manipulate and choose the cards to answer a particular question. In this book I will walk you through the processes of bonding with and cleaning your Tarot cards and calling in a Spirit Guide to assist you in your readings.

How do I know that the interpretations and messages offered in Tarot of The Lotus Circle *are valid?*

"Knowing" is a tough thing to explain. I know my name and home address. I have a state-issued driver's license for confirmation. I know the date and time, and there are numerous ways to confirm that. I also know things like math and spelling because they were taught to me by others who *knew* that information.

Whenever a skeptic asks me for an explanation of how crystals, Tarot cards and other tools of my trade work, I show them my cell phone. It has no visible wires running from it to a pole outside, yet I can use it to instantly talk to someone thousands of miles away. How? I don't know exactly, but I know it's not magic. I also know that crystals play a part in the transmission process. I don't need to know more than that. The fact is that I *know* a cell phone works because I experience the end result of that tool every day. The same reasoning applies to Tarot cards. We may not be able to "see" how the tool works, but I constantly see proof that it does when properly handled.

The Universe is filled with things we cannot see with our physical eyes. In fact, our eyes often make mistakes about the images they *can* capture. Sometimes, by closing our eyes to the physical world, we free ourselves to "see" things that are only visible through our mind's eye.

We were all given the gift of intuition to help us make good decisions, warn us of danger and inspire us to create new things. Unfortunately, many people have dismissed or blocked this gift for one reason or another. Please be assured that, regardless of how blocked or rusty your intuition is, by changing your belief of what is possible and doing some simple exercises, you can awaken the hibernating abilities in your mind.

In my book, *METAPHYSICAL FITNESS, Ten Commandments for Spiritual Being,* I guide you through the step-by-step process of living the life you were meant to be enjoying, including the utilization of all your God-given gifts. This book, *Tarot of The Lotus Circle,* will help you take a giant step to a more enlightened human existence.

The Lotus Circle deck, layout and interpretations are the result of nearly a decade of messages and visions I received from The Universe (feel free to substitute the term God, Infinite Spirit or so on). When my Spirit Guides directed me to share what I know about using cards to forecast events, they insisted the material be simple enough for novices to get helpful, thought-provoking answers to their questions. I was directed to modernize the images and interpretations, yet maintain respect for the basic meanings and traditional symbolism of the individual cards.

Also, you may note that I use the feminine, rather than masculine, pronouns in reference to non-specific people. This is a personal choice based on the fact that females outnumber males on this planet.

The process of channeling the information began for me when one Artist Spirit Guide held my hand to draw The Lotus Circle layout. Others showed me clear, detailed pictures that were to be used to illustrate the various meanings with familiar, contemporary scenes.

A number of different Guides gave me the worded messages. This occasionally took a while when they didn't all agree on the precise phrases to be used. They are, after all, from different times and space and have varying talents. For instance, the singer among them was rather pushy about using old song lyrics. If it had been up to her, the entire book would have been set to music! Through it all, my Guardian Angel, Isabel, watched over the proceedings to make sure I stayed on track and told me when it was time to go to bed.

At the same time as I was directed to create the *Tarot of The Lotus Circle*, I was given the assignment of introducing people to their Spirit Guides and directing readers to use their own intuition, along with metaphysical tools, to solve their problems. The Source of All That Is wants everyone to learn how to tap into the wisdom of The Universe whenever the need arises.

So, how do I know the messages in *Tarot of The Lotus Circle* are right? My Spirit Guides told me so. And I'm willing to bet that when you start working with your own Guides, you'll find that you also "know" some answers even before you pull a card and read its meaning.

HISTORY OF TAROT

It is not necessary to know the complete history of Tarot cards to use the *Tarot of The Lotus Circle*, but the following is a brief background for those of you who are curious about the origins of Tarot.

Throughout time on Earth, people have used a variety of tools in an attempt to divine the future. Something similar to a deck of Tarot cards was found in Egyptian tombs. The first playing cards with hearts, spades, clubs and diamonds were found in China in the tenth century, and in the west, a Swiss monk wrote a journal entry about a card game in 1377.

The first cards with Tarot-style pictures appeared in the mid-fifteenth century as part of a gift given to a Milanese Duke. That deck had twenty-two trump cards (Major Arcana) and fifty-six lesser cards (Minor Arcana) including sixteen nobility (Court) cards, which were divided into four suits, similar to contemporary Tarot decks, but it is not clear as to whether those cards were ever used for forecasting. However, it was in this time period that the possible origins of the word "tarot" may be found. That gift to the Duke was called *carte da trionfi* (card of triumphs), and about a century later, the cards were being referred to by another Italian word, *Tarocchi*, which has no confirmed etymology.

There is also the possibility that the word "tarot" was derived from Thoth, the Egyptian counterpart to the god of communication, Mercury. The Book of Thoth was said to have contained all knowledge, but was burned in the fires of the Alexandria libraries.

Despite all the conjectures, the word and spelling of the word "Tarot", as used today, is French.

Many students of Tarot also acknowledge a connection between the twenty-two Major Arcana, which tell of the steps of a human journey, and the Kabalistic Tree of Life, which has twenty-two intersecting paths of awareness.

If you are interested in delving further into the background, you might begin by researching the Hermetic Order of the Golden Dawn, a society formed in 1888, which was devoted to the study of the occult. Among their members were famous occultists and philosophers Aleister Crowley, Arthur Edward Waite and W. B. Yeats. Tarot cards were an important part of the Order's rituals. Their conclusions were the basis of Waite's deck, which was published by the Rider Company in 1910 and is generally considered to be the father of most of the Tarot cards used today.

Crowley's deck, titled The Book of Thoth, was not published until 1944 but is still considered a foundation deck. Although I do not agree with all the interpretations those esteemed gentlemen put forth—I find they lean too heavily toward the negative for today's culture—a true student of Tarot should at least be familiar with these two decks.

It is interesting to note that Waite made some changes in the ordering of the cards from earlier decks, based on his own and other interpretations made within the Order, with regard to the flow of the human journey being depicted. The Fool, which is 0 in the present-day Major Arcana and represents the beginner, was once the word used for the entire Lesser Arcana and then later, The Fool was set between the twentieth and twenty-first cards. Another change Waite made in the Major Arcana was that number 8, Strength, and number 11, Justice, were originally reversed.

There are also different terms for the four suits found in writings by various students of Tarot. For instance, Coins or Disks were the original terms used for what was later called Pentacles, and Wands were named Rods or Staves.

The bottom line is that there is no such thing as the definitive Tarot deck and no strict rules about the terms used. Basically, any deck of cards used for divination can be called a Tarot deck. The author and illustrator have the option of titling and interpreting the individual cards as they choose, depending on the intuitive messages they have received while in the process of designing the deck. It is up to the reader to select the deck that "speaks" to her personally.

Why an electronic book?

We live in the Information Age—an exciting time in the history of human civilization, in which technology rules supreme and continues to progress in leaps and bounds every minute of every day. For a multitude of reasons, more and more avid literary fans are opting to purchase e-books instead of paper books. The question from those not yet initiated into the world of electronic reading is simply: *Why?*

1. ***Price.*** An electronic title at Ellora's Cave Publishing and Cerridwen Press runs anywhere from 40% to 75% less than the cover price of the exact same title in paperback format. Why? Basic mathematics and cost. It is less expensive to publish an e-book (no paper and printing, no warehousing and shipping) than it is to publish a paperback, so the savings are passed along to the consumer.

2. ***Space.*** Running out of room in your house for your books? That is one worry you will never have with electronic books. For a low one-time cost, you can purchase a handheld device specifically designed for e-reading. Many e-readers have large, convenient screens for viewing. Better yet, hundreds of titles can be stored within your new library—on a single microchip. There are a variety of e-readers from different manufacturers. You can also read e-books on your PC or laptop computer. (Please note that Ellora's

Cave does not endorse any specific brands. You can check our websites at www.ellorascave.com or www.cerridwenpress.com for information we make available to new consumers.)

3. *Mobility.* Because your new e-library consists of only a microchip within a small, easily transportable e-reader, your entire cache of books can be taken with you wherever you go.

4. *Personal Viewing Preferences.* Are the words you are currently reading too small? Too large? Too... ANNOYING? Paperback books cannot be modified according to personal preferences, but e-books can.

5. *Instant Gratification.* Is it the middle of the night and all the bookstores near you are closed? Are you tired of waiting days, sometimes weeks, for bookstores to ship the novels you bought? Ellora's Cave Publishing sells instantaneous downloads twenty-four hours a day, seven days a week, every day of the year. Our webstore is never closed. Our e-book delivery system is 100% automated, meaning your order is filled as soon as you pay for it.

Those are a few of the top reasons why electronic books are replacing paperbacks for many avid readers.

As always, Ellora's Cave and Cerridwen Press welcome your questions and comments. We invite you to email us at Comments@ellorascave.com or write to us directly at Ellora's Cave Publishing Inc., 1056 Home Avenue, Akron, OH 44310-3502.

THE
☥ ELLORA'S CAVE ☥
LIBRARY

Stay up to date with Ellora's Cave Titles in
Print with our Quarterly Catalog.

TO RECIEVE A CATALOG,
SEND AN EMAIL WITH YOUR NAME
AND MAILING ADDRESS TO:

CATALOG@ELLORASCAVE.COM

OR SEND A LETTER OR POSTCARD
WITH YOUR MAILING ADDRESS TO:

CATALOG REQUEST
c/o ELLORA'S CAVE PUBLISHING, INC.
1056 HOME AVENUE
AKRON, OHIO 44310-3502

Entertainment ☼ *Education* ☼
Enlightenment ☼ *Empowerment*

The Lotus Circle is a multi-faceted, internet-based source for metaphysical books, products and services. The web store sells fiction and non-fiction books and new-age style products such as Tarot cards, rune stones, crystals, jewelry, incense, bags and scarves.

www.thelotuscircle.com